I0607454

Hearts in Danger

CHASE MY HEART

SANDRA CARMEL

ENTWINED PUBLISHING

Chase my Heart
ISBN # 978-1-80250-249-7
©Copyright Sandra Carmel 2025
Cover Art by Kelly Martin ©Copyright May 2025
Interior text design by Entwined Publishing
Published by Entice, an Entwined Publishing imprint

Published in 2025 by Entwined Publishing, United Kingdom.

Entwined Publishing is a division of Totally Entwined Group Limited.

CHASE MY HEART

Dedication

To all those who have fallen in love when they
least expected it.

Chapter One

You'll pay for putting innocent people away.

Chase Cassidy ignored the message sent to his public social media account. *Join the club.* Like he didn't get a similar sentiment most days since he'd made a name for himself. He almost laughed. Did these troublemaker trolls think they were the first? They weren't even close to the first and wouldn't be the last.

With his criminal prosecutor work, he regularly received death threats. And when he didn't, he questioned whether he was doing all he could, doing his job well enough. To the best of his ability, to the elite level he promised.

He checked his appearance in the staff toilets, whipped out a small spray bottle of his favorite expensive aftershave from his work satchel, then drove to the agency party, at an inner-city Melbourne bar. A celebration recognizing the Office of Public Prosecutions' efforts in convicting hardcore criminals above their estimated KPIs.

Great that they'd exceeded expectations, but KPIs weren't his driver. From what he'd seen, agencies came up with criteria to enhance their profits. To ensure they made money. And it made sense, but not when it came to people's lives.

What mattered most was putting the correct person away for their crime to reduce the risk to the broader population. It shouldn't have anything to do with money. And nothing to do with politics. But the two often went hand in greedy hand.

Since he started in the industry, he'd done well, quickly climbing past his colleagues. Over the years, he'd gotten a reputation for taking on tricky cases, and consistently making a conviction. And it raised his confidence to successfully do it again and again and again.

As a consequence, due to the respect he'd developed from his professionalism, plus high win rate commingled with a smattering of luck, the powers-that-be continued to listen to his ideas and requests, and support him. The positive outcomes had had a discernable flow-on effect that boosted his self-belief, making him feel invincible. Mostly.

Sure, he'd had some losses — that formed part of the reality of his job — but overall he'd excelled. His extroverted personality, passion for his work, and gift of the eloquent gab had played a huge part in his success.

With each appointed case, combined with his lifetime-learner mentality, he'd produced a recent winning streak — twenty successful convictions in a row — and had just won the highest profile criminal trial of his career. So he planned to cut loose and party. Assuming the circumstances supported him to let go. If required, he could always get an Uber home.

The second he stepped through the door of the small, stifling, overpriced bar, a close female colleague came straight over. She always seemed to know where he was, often requested his opinion and assistance with her work, and had a way of running into him throughout the day as well as at the local shops, like she'd installed a GPS tracker on him, notifying her of his every move.

At first he'd thought it coincidental, almost sort of sweet. But lately her clinginess had become almost claustrophobic. She wrapped him in what he wished was a grateful hug, but it had elements of so much more. Elements of attraction and desire, of hoping he'd think of her as a girlfriend rather than his coworker. Possibly both.

Chase pulled away as kindly as he could, without making a back-off-baby scene. "Anyone like a drink?" he yelled to the wider group, his voice hardly carrying past the pumping music.

With some effort, he noted their orders in his phone, ready and eager to escape the clutches of his predatory workmate.

Mixing business with casual sex never ended well. It caused nothing but complicated emotional crap. Add that complexity to someone who he suspected had an anxiety attachment style and accompanying obsessive tendencies and…disaster.

In his earlier, super carefree days he'd tried dating work colleagues and suffered the cock-blocking consequences. But, thankfully, he'd learned from experience, and made sure he never traveled that precarious path again.

Somehow, he extricated himself from his clingy coworker's clutches and headed to the dark red neon-lit bar and waited in the five-deep queue. She didn't follow, thank fuck.

Not that she wasn't a nice girl. She seemed lovely. Sweet, friendly, innocent. Pretty, polite, but totally not his type. Too…serious, suffocating. Young. And he imagined ambitious too. Hooking up with him could bolster her professional opportunities, her pay. Too many reasons added up to staying away from interacting with the woman privately.

A celebratory, no-strings-attached fuck would go down a treat, but not with any of his workmates. No fucking way. A fun fuck was one thing, but fucking up his career was quite another. Not even close to worth it.

As it stood, he carefully scrutinized his hook-ups these days, because for too many women in the past, it meant more. Even though they assured him it didn't. Even though he made it clear from the outset he had no interest in commitment.

He wasn't against long-term relationships per se, he just hadn't met anyone who came anywhere in the vicinity of changing his mind from his current love-'em-and-leave-'em lifestyle. Add the political, office environment and *no*. No. Mixing business with short-term pleasure never had the desired result. For either person.

Chase scanned the crowded venue for unattached, non-work-related females, and spotted some possible prospects. It'd been a while since his last dalliance, but he'd have to suss them and their thinking out first.

Yeah, he loved women, loved a good fuck, but not something serious…unless the lady met his stringent criteria. They needed to connect across all planes — physical, mental, emotional, spiritual, intellectual.

He'd thought his best friend, Alex, had similar sentiments, that they were brothers in eternal bachelorhood, but then he'd gone and clicked with Chase's sister, Sage. Married her.

And he couldn't fault the guy. Sage was fucking awesome. The sweetest, funniest, most intelligent woman. His friend had fucking fantastic taste. Chase considered Sage a prize to any person, and his mate obviously agreed. And yeah, okay, they might both be a little biased.

Chase shuffled forward, jostled by intoxicated patrons, and those hoping to grab a drink to escape. They all had that in common. A little sip to numb the senses, to chill after a challenging week.

Hopefully with Alex's new business and Sage's psychology practice, they hadn't been too busy to have some fun. His sister constantly focused on doing all she could to attain exceptional outcomes for her clients, friends and family. Fucking admirable. Some would argue more admirable than his work. Though, he liked to believe he helped protect broader society.

The loud music, combined with people singing and dancing around him—a mish-mash of aftershaves and perfumes assaulting his senses—made it impossible to hear more than a few snippets of conversation. He didn't intend to eavesdrop but it proved helpful on occasion. For work, for his personal life.

He loosened his tie, slid it from around his perspiring neck and shoved it in his pants pocket. He'd love to discard his jacket as well but, for the moment, he'd have to settle for undoing the top few buttons of his shirt.

His phone vibrated, the screen lighting up with a text message. He unlocked it and...a congratulations message from Sage. His sis had tuned right into his thoughts, as though she had some sort of super-sensitive ESP.

He typed a quick *thank you* and promised to catch up with her soon.

Unlike most brothers, he'd tried to evaluate things with perspective rather than going all over-protective when she and Alex had gotten together. He trusted Sage and his best mate, respected both their decisions, so had refused to resort to primitive, authoritarian behavior. They were adults and knew what they were doing, what best suited each other.

Their relationship remained between them. It had nothing to directly do with him. His role stretched to supportive brother and friend. That's all. Coming down hard on either of them with a do-as-I-say-not-as-I-do approach would have only incited rebellion and ended in a total shitshow.

Ultimately, he loved, valued and appreciated his best friend but still kept his well-trained eyes and ears on him to make sure he wouldn't screw over his beloved sister. Even in the slightest way.

Overall, he backed the relationship between them. In fact, he'd always believed they shared a special connection, though it had taken them several years to finally work out what everyone else could see clearly.

Their goals and dreams and desires had to align, and they well and truly did, going by their constant happy glow. Which was fantastic, but the sickeningly saccharine I-love-you-so-much stuff, at times, got grating.

Chase fiddled with his sapphire-and-platinum cufflinks—a graduation gift from his now deceased parents—adjusted his fitted jacket, and stepped up to the front of the queue. Why had he agreed to come again?

Because he'd wanted to celebrate, but freely. He didn't need the extra stress of workmates expecting more, of disappointment and hurt if he chose to go home with someone else.

Pursuing his flirty teammate, even if he was interested, was the stuff of nightmares as far as he'd seen, and experienced.

The last thing he needed was a possible bunny boiler to add to his everyday worklist of disgruntled rapists and murderers. In fact, he almost feared scorned women more.

Obsessive passion created extreme thinking, extreme actions. Nothing he wanted to be a part of, a situation requiring a shit-ton of distance. For everyone's wellbeing, and the wellbeing of the workplace.

He'd buy his colleagues their drinks, speak some socially acceptable small talk, and head off before alcohol further impaired people's judgments. His too.

Chase ordered and paid, and loaded up a tray, carrying it over to the female-dominated group, the blaring music thumping in his chest, the white and red laser lights flashing across the crowd.

Each person selected their poison, and he deposited the tray on a nearby table, grabbed his gin and tonic and took a sip.

"How's Sage?" A tentative woman's voice broke through his introspective thoughts.

He glanced to his side and smiled at the young blonde secretary from his office. Somewhat sincere, mostly forced, but a networking requirement. "She's going well, thank you."

Chase gulped down more of his drink. Disillusioned, cynical, frustrated. So unlike his usual Mr. Positive attitude. Maybe the recent threats had impacted on him more than he'd realized.

A guy slapped him on the back. "Great work, mate, putting Mike away. He deserves to die in jail." Before Chase could reply, the stranger disappeared into the throng of people gyrating on the dance floor.

All the glory and increased status Chase had achieved since he stepped into his new head prosecutor role a year ago had him regularly making the newspaper and social media articles.

He'd worked hard to get there, really hard, through all sorts of adversity—his parents' untimely deaths, Sage's stalking situation, his myriad of unfulfilled relationships—and had crossed the number one thing off his bucket list.

His promotion had happened right before his car accident, Sage's confirmation of her relationship with Alex, and the conviction of her stalker. So many key changes in a short time.

Chase placed his empty glass on the closest high table and turned to go.

"Did— Ah...you're not leaving?" The PA touched his arm, her eyes practically pleading.

Chase fixed his best suave, sophisticated, soothing smile onto his face. "Not yet. Let's do the rounds." Damn. It was the easiest, least argumentative option. Because, yeah, he didn't want to get into the whole why-he-didn't-want-to-date-her thing.

The facts were this girl had an I-want-to-marry-you tattoo virtually etched onto her forehead. Her intention, her hope, her wish, radiated into her aura like an iridescent choose-me sign.

His instinct had him wanting to run for the door. Run as far away as possible. Not that she wasn't nice too. Like his clingy coworker. But he didn't do nice.

Impulsivity drove him to stop overthinking and continue to enjoy each and every unique moment, but zeroing in on a quick fix wasn't worth the trouble. Why sacrifice what he desired?

He'd rather be on his own than in an unsuitable, unsatisfying union, whether it be for a night, a week or a month. Any poorly chosen partnership could potentially cost him his career.

Chase worked his way around the group, with the PA as his shadow, his other clingy colleague giving him daggers, while he tried to act unaffected, doing the whole schmoozy thing. So much harder with the noise and only one drink, but he needed to be sober to drive home and ensure he didn't make an alcohol-infused regrettable decision. He tugged on his blue suit sleeves until he couldn't stand the superficial chit chat much longer.

Within fifteen minutes he said his goodbyes— charming grin plastered onto his face plus the accompanying socially acceptable handshakes and air kisses—and slipped out of the door without hassle. Without any tagalongs, without an unwelcome proposition.

With his ears ringing like tolling bells, he strode past the crowd of people eager to enter the establishment, and weaved his way through the sea of cars in the parking lot. Pressing the button on the keyless entry fob in his front pocket clicked open the doors of his McLaren 720S upon his approach. His first big, highly valued, purchase since he'd joined the prosecution team.

Actually, his high-end, luxury vehicle didn't just appeal to him, or attract women. Other men fucking loved it too. Maybe more so. They struggled not to drool, not to go all fan boy. Both sexes stopped him all the time to talk about its features and performance. But right now, he didn't have the patience. He needed to drive to his place, uninterrupted, and chill.

He'd been at work since before seven a.m., was absolutely buggered, and required a shower, a relaxing night cap, some self-pleasure, then sleep. All in that exact order.

"Chase!"

He froze. Not the sycophant secretary. His clingy colleague, her voice distinguishable over the loud, muffled music. What did she want? Fingers fucking crossed it had nothing to do with any sort of work emergency.

He forced a smile onto his lips and faced the woman. "What's up?"

She flicked her flaming red hair off her shoulder and tugged at her dress. "We didn't really get to talk."

"About?"

"Non-work stuff, personal interests, passions." She stepped right up to him until their bodies almost touched, her cheeks flushed.

Oh no. He subtly stepped back, his butt hitting the driver's side door. *Cornered.* "It's hard to get into anything in depth when you can hardly hear yourself think."

She laughed, reached up and ran her hand along the length of his lapel. "True. Maybe we should go somewhere quiet?"

"Sorry, I can't. I really need to get going."

"Oh, come on. Stay and have some fun. My place is only a couple of blocks away." Her hand hovered way too close to his crotch.

"I don't think that's a good idea."

"Why not? We'd just be letting off some built-up steam."

"I don't like to blur the lines between work and my personal life. It creates awkwardness and unnecessary complications."

"Not always. Not when both parties are emotionally mature adults who understand and stick to the agreed terms."

The idea sounded great, infallible, but it rarely played out like that in practice. Emotions had a way of clouding reason, providing a person with excuses as to why it was different in this instance. Or highlighted they each had varying views on the *agreement*. "I value and appreciate our professional relationship too much to risk ruining it."

"Maybe I should make sure you get fired then," she said with a sassy smile, her gaze dipping to his lips, then straight back to his eyes.

She wouldn't go to that extent, would she? But who knew what a scorned person would do? Didn't matter. He could back himself as long as he didn't give her anything to use against him.

Trying to make light of the situation, he chuckled, wracking his brain for the right combination of words to gently but firmly shut down the conversation. Let her know he wouldn't reconsider. "We can have a chat in the lunchroom tomorrow."

She wrinkled her nose and pouted. "Not quite what I had in mind."

No, he bet it wasn't. "I really need to get moving."

"I suppose I should let you go then." She hesitated, then stepped back and wrapped her arms around herself, her smile no longer reaching her eyes.

"See you in the morning."

She nodded, turned and hurried back to the bar, figurative tail between her legs.

He dropped into the driver's seat, started the car and sighed. *Narrow bloody escape.* Crisis temporarily averted. Hopefully their little discussion didn't negatively impact their working relationship or else he might have to look for another job.

Chase reached his home within ten minutes and pressed the remote to open the large wrought-iron gates. Closing them behind him, he drove along the solar lit driveway, highlighting the mix of trees, bush and native flowers.

He parked in the garage, dove under the descending roller door, and approached the front entrance of his house.

Ajar? *What the fuck?* How come the alarm hadn't gone off? Had someone disabled it and broken in, or had he forgotten to activate it and not closed the front door properly?

He'd never slackened off when it came to setting the alarm or locking up. If anything, he'd shown over-vigilance, over-cautiousness, one-hundred-and-fifty percent reliability. Except he'd had an urgent call that morning and had still been on the phone when he'd rushed out.

With his heart thudding incessantly in his chest, loud enough for the neighbors to hear, he peeked into the front yard, then using his shoulder, nudged the heavy wooden door, swinging it wide, the squeak — if not his raucous heartbeat — announcing his arrival. Hopefully, if anyone had broken in, they'd have departed by now. Fingers fucking crossed.

Work bag still slung over his shoulder, he locked the door and scanned the foyer. The alarm display flashed. The power must have gone out. He flicked on his smartphone torch and carefully crept through the bottom level of his home. No noise. No obvious break-in. Nothing of significance missing from what he'd observed. No concern for his safety. Or so he fucking hoped.

The microwave and oven clocks flashed in the kitchen. An electrical interruption of some sort had definitely occurred.

Next he scaled the stairs to the upper level. No mess, everything in its place, and nothing absent, as far as he could see. However, he didn't keep anything of much worth in the house in order to reduce his risk of loss in this exact scenario. Most of his valuables he'd locked up in a safe deposit box in one of the big banks in town.

Chase dumped his satchel and plonked onto his bed, suddenly super weary. He took a big breath and gathered himself, collected a tracksuit from his cupboard and had a quick shower.

Afterward, he returned downstairs, reset the alarm, ready to reactivate it on the way to bed, and made a beeline to his bar. He poured himself a shot of gin, and added a splash of soda water and a slice of lemon. He'd always preferred it over the standard lime.

He sank onto his soft leather recliner, pressed the remote control to lift his feet then turned on the TV, and had a few sips of his drink. When he was done, for the moment, he put the glass in the cup holder in the armrest.

His usual comfy, wind-down position but he didn't have the inclination to concentrate on anything. His mind wandered all over the place. He couldn't rally the required attention, he couldn't be fucked. In every sense of the word.

He sigh-groaned and dropped his face into his fidgety hands. Tomorrow he'd need to discuss taking on a new case, whether he assessed himself as ready or not, and aim to continue his amazing success rate. Aim to give the victims a voice. For justice. One of the main reasons he'd remained driven to the fuck.

His phone rang, setting off an eruption of stress in his stomach. What if it was his clingy colleague or the over-eager department secretary wanting to give their propositions a second shot after downing some more liquid courage? But it could also be Sage or Alex, so he couldn't ignore the call. They might need his help.

He whipped his phone out of his sweatpants pocket. Alex's picture filled the screen so he answered. "Everything all right?"

"Relax, mate. All good. I'm not interrupting anything am I?"

"No."

"You alone?"

"Yeah."

"My deepest condolences." Alex's smart-ass laugh drifted down the phone line. "I'm sure you'll rectify the situation soon, going by your history."

He hoped so. He hadn't had any intimate female company for several weeks. The Mike DeSalvo case had taken up most of his work and spare time for months. "Anyway, I'm sure you didn't call to talk about my love life." *Or current lack of it.*

"I actually rang to congratulate you on your big win. But I'm happy to speak about women if you want to."

"Thanks. Nothing to report on the lady front at the moment, but it's great to get scumbags like Mike off the streets."

"Absolutely. Are you having any holidays? Any plans to go up to the cabin?"

"No holiday, no cabin, no rest for the wicked." Chase laughed.

"A word of unsolicited advice." Alex's usually sarcastic, smart-ass tone turned super serious. "At least allow for a long weekend before you burn out, before your body breaks down and you're forced to take leave. Believe me, it happens, and usually when you're the least prepared." Alex knew all about that, unrelenting PTSD having led to his premature discharge from the military.

"I hear you. I promise I'll schedule in a few days away soon."

"Good. Oh, and you should drop by the office. It's almost all set up. I've recruited some top-notch security staff and am now focused on filling the remaining few roles."

"Fantastic. I'll aim to swing by in the next week or two." He tried to stifle a yawn. "Anyway, I need to get to bed. Say hi to Sage."

"Will do.

Chase hung up, switched off the TV and sat in the cold silence. The fact he couldn't find time for a fuck reinforced he'd poured too much energy into work. He needed to reprioritize to achieve better work-life balance without compromising on results.

Using the remote to adjust his chair into a sitting position, Chase propelled off the couch and headed to his bedroom. He hoped local citizens, and those Australia-wide, appreciated his skills, his silver-tongued style because that combo prevented further problems, got criminals convicted. Some residents might even see him as a community-centric crusader, a society superhero.

Chapter Two

Physically recovered from her recent work-related assault, police detective Lexie Stark returned to the station, dressed in her professional attire — black jeans, black top, black jacket, black hair slicked back in a low bun — a packet of mints always in her pocket, ready and waiting to resume her role in the field.

Helping people, the community, had always been her passion. Ensuring equity, fairness, justice. She straightened out her plain-clothed uniform, took a slow, steady breath, walked out of the elevator and straight through the chaotic, overly air-conditioned, open-plan office to her boss's door. She knocked, and the rowdy floor went silent.

She glimpsed over her shoulder, the fluorescent globes casting a stark, intense, blue-tinged light over the stale, sardine-style space, her colleagues frozen in place, their curious, gossipy eyes on her.

She'd thought they were supportive, on her side, but would they come to her aid when it mattered? Her own fiancé hadn't. And she had no close family or friends to rely on for financial or emotional assistance.

Lexie had an older brother but he lived in a hippy-style commune and she hardly saw or spoke to him. Her work 'mates' had the added should-they-network versus cut-out-the-competition conflict to meet their own career goals.

The door squeaked and she twisted her head to meet her manager's dour expression. He gestured for her to enter his office. "Lexie, good to see you." His lips twitched with an insincere smile. He shut them into the compact, closet-like room. "Take a seat."

She did, her superior turning his back and standing by the dirty window overlooking the car park. Not a good sign. A shit sign, from what she'd seen. Her super-tingly, Spidey senses crawled up her spine, setting the alarm bells off in her head to high-alert.

She attempted to go into the Zen zone, psychologically prepare herself for the absolute worst, career-wise, hoping her negative mindset, her worries — still stemming from the crossover into her personal life — wouldn't eventuate. In this instance, she'd like nothing better than to be proven wrong.

Her boss swung around, focusing his beady, unsure eyes on her face. "You know the department love and respect you…"

But… Unequivocally impossible not to notice. The true meaning as loud and insistent as fireworks blasting the message across the night sky.

"However, we also need to accommodate new recruits." As in, government contracts pressed the department to fulfill funding accreditation requirements and take newbies onboard, especially those who wouldn't question anything, would toe the line to move up the ladder.

Those who'd keep quiet and do as they were told, which assisted the agency to achieve their own long-term agenda. The entrenched, well-established boys' club. Covert but insidious. Fucking sickening. The organization basically wanted *yes*, we'll-do-your-bidding people.

"This whole thing was a massive close call. You need to look after yourself. A fresh focus is required to guarantee the safest outcome going forward. And I'll fully support your transition."

"Excuse me? Transition to what? Did you even read my incident report, my suggestions for improving processes across the board, ideas to enhance everyone's safety and efficiency?"

She bit back her mounting frustration. "You might not have had time, I understand that you're busy, I get it, but you haven't even asked how I am, what I need, what my thoughts are to ensure the safest, most efficient working conditions for everyone."

"Of course I've read it." Her boss, typically non-committal, dance-around-the-subject, deflect wherever possible — Mr. Ultimate Politician — shoved his fingers through his receding hair, fully flustered but pretending to be fine. "How *are* you?"

Fucking annoyed. Fucking frustrated. Fucking disappointed. "Ready to return." She'd worked her ass off to secure a job in the highly male-dominated field only to be questioned at every single turn, at double the instance of her male colleagues, and her thoughts and feelings undermined.

Lexie had entered the police force with wide-eyed optimism. But she'd soon understood the skewed environment, that her idealism was just that — ideal. She'd realized she needed to work harder to make her mark, to show her worth, and she had — even though she shouldn't have had to prove anything more than her fellow workmates.

She'd done it unfailingly, even when something was far from her fault. Followed protocol to the absolute letter of the law because it resonated with her over and above the prejudice.

Then, the moment it didn't suit, the moment it drew negative attention to the precinct, she became the scapegoat, she needed to suffer the career-ending consequences.

What she needed, required, desired for everyone's best interests was well and truly buried under the very indoctrinated carpet. The bureaucracy, the in-house regulations, the political situation all had an influence, and were all out of her control.

"Like I said, I can help." He stepped toward her and reached for her arm. She flinched and scooted back in her chair, interlocking her fingers and holding her hands close to her body. As in, *don't you dare touch me.*

Lexie glared at the man she'd lost every ounce of respect for. "Don't feed me bullshit. Don't try and appease me. I was hurt in the line of duty and it's fucking upsetting to hear my own squad no longer believes in me."

She shook her head and huffed. "I fucking did everything for you, my partner, this fucking department, only to have you question me and my judgment? I've followed all the procedures, all the protocols. Achieved consistently exceptional results. Look it up.

"Have you disciplined any of my male counterparts who've been injured in the line of duty? No. They've all still retained their positions without question. Some of them have fucked up majorly and haven't had anywhere near my level of scrutiny, my level of punishment. Some have even been promoted."

Entering into a testosterone-dominated, cliquey environment, how could she have ever thought things would be fair? That if she worked hard, had excellent arrest results she'd be considered an equal.

"If it wasn't for my investigative work and insights, you wouldn't have the current high conviction rates." Lexie crossed her arms and stared at the weak little company man standing in front of her, tangled in red tape.

Oh yeah, easy for the guy to speak shit when backed financially, when backed by his high-end buddies who also had a finger in the political pie.

But other than that, when she, a grass-roots worker, questioned his overarching opinions, his scruples, plus those of the elite, higher echelons of the police force, they held up a huge *keep out* sign. And proved that trespassers would definitely be prosecuted...in some way or another.

"I can assure you that everyone is assessed based on their individual circumstances and abilities. It has nothing at all to do with gender."

Or nepotism, or favors, right? Sure thing.

"Your hard work and consistent efforts, along with my endorsement, have convinced my superiors to retain you, but in a more suitable capacity. A position where you can use your full gamut of expertise without putting you physically at risk."

As in gagged, behind-the-scenes, stuck in the office in front of a computer? As in providing a significantly reduced ability to draw attention to the precinct, to cause trouble?

"Given what's happened, I believe you need a positive sideways shift, so I'm taking you off patrol, off the streets. Your skills are much better suited to an admin-research role."

What a fucking crock! He'd made an executive decision without even consulting her about what she enjoyed, without factoring in her career goals. She virtually vibrated with repressed anger, struggling to sit still. She wanted to jump up, grab the guy's shirt collar and pin him against the wall until he could see sense.

So infuriating having her hands figuratively tied. Because she didn't have the contacts, the network support, she couldn't do a fucking thing about it. She'd be suppressed, smothered, blocked at every step.

From his well-rehearsed, overt, cowardly words, the department had met the minimum work-requirement criteria, and relegated her to a zero hands-on area.

Something, anything, as long as the organization did their duty and found a 'safe', shut-her-down, spot. Heaven forbid she might request stress leave or additional pay given the added OH&S risk of her previous occupation. Heaven-fucking-forbid she might relay some facts and kick up a fuss.

Her manager walked to his desk and fumbled through a pile of paper, then checked his computer screen. "You've been reassigned to level three. I'll email through further details as soon as I have them."

Level three? She knew that all too well. That's where they sent cops to die., Not literally, but from a career perspective. Unsurprising that they'd repurposed her into a dreaded desk-jockey job.

Just the idea had her clenching and gnawing her teeth together. She slammed her fist into her hand, over and over. Being the only woman who'd successfully gotten into the select group had made her proud. Beforehand. Now they wanted to take the hard-won privilege, that accolade, away from her. Had made it almost impossible for her to climb the prestigious ranks.

She'd given up a lot—friends, family, potential and actual boyfriends, a fiancé—had had to work doubly as hard as any of the men to even get a look in to the super-elite setting. And because of an unfortunate circumstance beyond her control, she had to relocate to a downgraded role? What the fricking fuck?

He swallowed, and stared at her punching, fisted hand, stress practically radiating out of his every pore.

Lexie stopped, and tried to contain the remaining anger circulating like an uncontrollable bushfire through her veins. She clenched her hands and pressed her lips together.

Arguing wouldn't help. Wouldn't get her the outcome she desired. She didn't want to work in some second-class, shit-eating job. So she did the only other thing she could do.

"Sitting at a desk is not why I chose law enforcement. But seeing I haven't been given the stamp of approval to return to what I love, I can't continue. With incredible sadness"—and a fuck-ton of fury—"I submit my verbal resignation."

"What? No. Wait—"

She held up her hand in a stop-right-there gesture. "I'll email you my official letter later today or tomorrow." No matter what he said , he couldn't convince her to stay. His words, his body language, his general behavior all reinforced the prejudicial environment. One she now accepted she'd never had a hope of entering, of attaining equal membership in.

Seething, annoyed and frustrated at the injustice, but adamant not to show any weakness, she walked away, each and every step slow and measured. She wanted to stomp and scream and swear but, fuck them. Fuck them all.

With her teeth firmly clamped together, she unlocked her car, sat in the driver's seat and swung the door closed with controlled force. She propped her arms onto the steering wheel and leaned into it, sucking in much needed gulps of fresh air.

Maybe sustaining an injury had been for the best. It had gotten her away from a toxic work environment, as well as preventing her from making a massive life-changing mistake in her personal life.

Her ex-fiancé had well and truly revealed his compromised cards, the full extent of his true colors when it counted. Hadn't allowed any buffer, hadn't stood by her, hadn't shown any real love or respect. Hadn't let her explain.

Initially she'd broken down, been beside herself. Lost, heartbroken, bereft, but not anymore, not in the scheme of things... Fuck anyone who planned to screw her over with their shit. She no longer had time for it in her personal or professional life.

She believed in herself, what she could do, how she could assist society, and she intended to find a role that appreciated what she had to offer. Her inner confidence created a sense of certainty that she'd find something she aligned with. Like attracted like, right? The laws of physics.

She started up the car, backed out of the parking spot and drove home.

Good riddance to her old job. Good riddance to her selfish, unsupportive ex-fiancé. His actions demonstrated he hadn't respected her or what she had to offer. The guy was full of bullshit. He knew how to talk, charmed women with his words. Could spout the most-believable lip-service crap, rarely following it up with action.

In her experience, no matter what he said, he wasn't and never would be honest, fully trustworthy, entirely redeemable.

After her ex-partner's decision to end their relationship at the most crucial, difficult time, she'd learned to stay far, far away from shit-talkers.

His departure was a benefit, really. She'd seen her ex's character laid bare before it was too late. If she reviewed it from a positive perspective, she'd thank him for teaching her an extremely important lesson — be careful who you lie with or you may wake up with an infestation of fleas.

She stopped at a red light.

Having experienced it firsthand, she'd hopefully recognize the behavior early on, next time. And if she didn't, she'd break up with the prick, as soon as practically possible.

The light turned green and Lexie continued on her journey home. She'd had her fun, her experimental period, her short-term hook-ups, her one-night stands but she'd moved past that thinking.

Refused to return there, even after a failed engagement. She'd reached a point where, as clichéd as it sounded, she wanted to settle down with a man who cared, who loved her as much as she loved him.

No more flings, no more game playing, no more emotional angst. Not some compromise, not some interim option until one or both of them found someone 'better'. Ultimately, she wouldn't enter into a situation where either of them strung each other along.

She sighed, eager to retreat into the safety and comfort of her flat, her sanctuary, part of her determined to wallow and part of her not wanting to give the department dicks the satisfaction.

The rest of the trip, where-to-from-here thoughts bounced around her brain. Firstly, she had to sign up to an employment site and start sifting through possibilities. She needed to get back on the work horse before she descended into depression.

Within ten minutes, she pulled up at her apartment, strode inside and slammed the door, all her pent-up energy desperate to express itself, demanding an outlet. She slumped onto the couch and turned on the TV. Not to watch, more as background noise, a much-needed distraction.

Lexie rubbed her moist eyes, then snatched her cell phone from the back pocket of her black jeans. She navigated onto a job seeker website, entered her parameters and scrolled and scrolled and scrolled.

Same fucking shit. Over and fucking over. She almost chucked her mobile across the room. But aggression wouldn't solve her issue. Nor would smashing her phone. She needed it to find and secure her next occupational opportunity. Especially now that she no longer had a landline. No longer had secure employment.

Other than her laptop, her phone was her only direct connection to the ever-sprawling outside world. Essentially her mobile acted as a mini, accessible computer, one she could draw on whenever she needed it, available straight out of her pocket or handbag.

Not for banking, never for banking. Smartphones and computers were way too easy to hack these days. Sure, having a separate set up reduced convenience but she'd rather be slightly put out and retain her capital. So she'd invested in a separate burner phone, purely for financial purposes, including online purchases, with super-tight security.

With no job hits after thirty minutes, she put her everyday phone on to charge, and ordered a pizza from her favorite local gourmet place. She shed her contaminated clothes, showered, and shrugged on her black dressing gown, just in time for her door-delivered dinner to arrive.

Lexie got comfy on her two-seater couch, pizza box balanced on her lap, and bit into the first slice of her vegetarian concoction with added ham, pineapple and anchovies. *De-lic-ious*. Just what she'd needed. The quintessential comfort food.

She could never order straight off a menu. According to others, she had unique, 'weird', tastes. But the combination worked for her, which was all that currently mattered. When she had to share a meal, she could compromise. Like she had for years. Right now, she'd enjoy eating whatever she wanted...within reason. If she endeavored to find another active role, she needed to remain fit, agile and healthy.

With the beginnings of a carb coma, she clicked into the job seeker app again and restarted her search for suitable occupations, ones that resonated with her beliefs, her fight for fairness, her life view. Maybe more businesses had added new ads in the interim, provided info on something that piqued her interest.

Flipping from job to job within her nominated field, and finding nothing, she refreshed her search. More scrolling, more reading, more refinement of factors, and nothing, nothing, nothing. WorkCover still paid her partial compensation, but that would soon cease. She needed a new position as soon as feasibly possible.

Considering the short timeframe, she couldn't afford to be too picky. She could always start somewhere, keep searching, then move to another more rewarding option.

She was just about to give up when the cursor blinked right over the top of something promising — the smallest little advertisement for a new protection company, Solve Security, located nearby. Within walking distance.

A range of jobs were available for ex-military, ex-police-force, and ex-service employees, including bodyguard, protection-style work. The kind of profession she had more than a burning desire to enter, and was more than equipped to do. A career she'd thrive in, embrace, love. Saving others while saving herself.

She clicked into the job description for further details. The ad specified that the employer would provide an equal opportunity establishment, ensuring award rates and conditions, which reinforced her initial positive assumption, giving her a great vibe about the place.

Lexie trawled through her files to find her last job application and updated the cover letter, her key performance indicators, and her CV. Once she'd read over her revised documents, checking for typos, spelling and grammatical errors, she immediately applied to the listed email address for Solve Security.

Now all she had to do was wait.

Chapter Three

Expect vengeance.
Your time will come.
Denial won't prevent death.

Chase shoved his fingers through his hair and tried to stop trembling. The recent string of comments in his public messenger app were the first that had gotten to him. Really gotten to him, had him totally off kilter. Normally he'd receive the odd crazy remark, but not a persistent barrage of threats from what appeared to be the same person.

His pulse raced, cold sweat beaded on his back, and tension gripped his stomach like an unforgiving fist. Now he knew, on a full-on visceral level, how his sister, Sage, had felt.

This die-hard spew of threatening words had forced him to take things seriously. He spun his office chair around, pushed it into recline, and stared out at the busy Melbourne city streets below, distractedly twisting his signature sapphire-and-platinum cufflinks. Unable to sit still.

Chase craved a coffee but it would only exacerbate his twitchy, agitated symptoms. He should prepare for his next court case but he couldn't concentrate. He had to do something to ease his mind, give him focus, give him some idea about the best course of action.

Normally he charmed his way out of difficult situations but for once, his appearance and suave, sophisticated persona wouldn't work. This time, he needed help, to at least run it by his best friend and brother-in-law, Alex.

Using his broad base of skills, and eager to feel purposeful after leaving the armed forces, Alex had recently started a security firm. Being ex-military, and still connected with key contacts in the field, he'd know what to do, how best to direct him. He'd saved Sage's life…though Chase's sister argued she equally contributed to capturing her stalker.

Up until now, Chase had resisted reporting anything to the police. Up until now he'd stayed complacent, pretty much desensitized. Untouchable. Not anymore. Things had gotten scarily serious. Had taken a dangerous detour.

Unlike the previous threats, the most recent ones had practically palpable venom. They felt like the person might literally take things further. Physically target Chase. Or his sister, Sage. Or Alex. Anyone close to him. He needed to let them know so they were prepared.

He couldn't put his best mate or his sister at increased risk, didn't want to blindside them, not after Sage had only just recovered. They'd both more than paid their dues. Thank fuck he had no other living family, no one else he had to consider.

Right. He could sit and stew or he could act. And the sooner he took action, the absolute better.

Chase snatched his mobile off the desk and speed-dialed Alex.

"What's up?"

"What makes you think something's wrong?"

"Your response just confirmed it." He could hear the *gotcha* tone in his friend's voice.

Chase could argue—he fucking loved arguing, excelled at it, did it for a living. But what was the point? Alex had seen through him, always had, and he needed to warn his best mate, plus he needed some answers. Both of them probably did at this point. He had to cut to the proverbial chase. "I've had a few death threats."

"What? Have you told the police?" Alex's what-the-fuck voice practically barked down the phone line. Firm, concerned, unyielding.

"Not yet." He cringed as he said it.

A frustrated hiss-sigh filtered through to Chase's ear. "Why?" Restraint echoed in Alex's tone, like he'd tried to hold back his concerns, keep the conversation calm, had clamped his teeth together to prevent a well-meaning lecture, an are-you-crazy tirade.

Chase let out a stressed, bottled-up breath. "At first I didn't think the person was serious. Well, not serious enough to act."

He hadn't wanted to worry anyone or expand the assailant's pool of people to pick from to possibly scare, injure, kill, adding immeasurable, unrecoverable hurt to Chase's already unsettled psyche.

"From this point forward, you need to report anything odd. And that's a demand not a request. Call the cops, even if you don't believe it poses much danger. In these matters you can't be subjective. You need to log the details and let law enforcement investigate. Let the specialists in the field make the final decision based on facts."

Alex huffed out a bothered, tough-love breath. "Why the fuck didn't you at least tell *me*? Why did you wait until now? I could have done something. I could have helped de-escalate the situation."

Could he? Really? Too late now to test his mate's negotiator skills.

Was Alex offended, disappointed because Chase hadn't confided in him, his best friend, or was it because he worried about him, and by association, Sage's safety? Probably all of the above? His brother-in-law was a born protector.

"Death threats are part of my *normal* so I didn't think anything of it." *Initially.* Recently he'd thought too much about the back catalogue of unnerving statements, but no way would he admit that—he'd set Alex off on an even larger well-intentioned but painful rant.

His mate took a breath to speak but Chase cut him off. "I know it's an excuse. I should have said something, but I guess I'd gone into avoidance. If I had a redo, I'd respond differently. But you know now, and I'm asking for your highly valued expertise."

"Luckily for you, and others, nothing serious happened."

"I know. I get it. You don't need to ram the point home any harder. I understand and wholeheartedly agree. I'll be more mindful from this point forward."

Chase wouldn't make the same, even similar, mistake again. Hoped he lived long enough to never have to contemplate it in the future, but he might, if he stayed working in his prosecutor role. Pissing people off kind of came with the territory.

Alex blew out a frustrated-sounding sigh. "What makes the threats different this time?"

Thank fuck his switched-on friend had seen the importance of shifting the conversation forward. Moving from lecture mode to solution focused.

"Normally the offhand comments come from a range of people, but in this instance, they've originated from the same account. So I'm assuming they're from the same person. A couple of guys I put away in the past have recently been released on good behavior — George Ulysses and Damien Bacia — so it could be connected to them but — "

"But what? No more hiding shit. I need you to be as upfront and clear as possible. No more wasting time fucking around. Got it?"

"Yeah." Loud and extremely fucking clear. Normally he didn't take well to people telling him what to do, but he loved, respected and appreciated Alex and his opinion, trusted the man with his life. "I actually think the taunts are linked to Mike DeSalvo." Or so his gut insisted.

"The aggravated-assault rapist? The high-profile case you just won?"

"That's the one." The guy he'd put away for twenty-five years.

"Why him? How him? He's incarcerated."

"He is. So it can't be him directly, but he may have found a way to outsource. Call it instinct, but I feel like he's behind this, or in collusion with someone somehow. Though, I don't have any definite data, and am unaware of any known close contacts in the community."

"Better than nothing," Alex murmured.

Chase could picture him sitting at his desk, staring at his computer tablet, scratching his scruff, trying to think of where to start investigating, the best way to help.

"Send me every one of the person's threatening communications and I'll try to pinpoint their location. See if they link with those offenders in any way."

"Okay. But I doubt they're that stupid. I doubt they'd send anything from a traceable phone or email or social media account."

"I doubt it too, but it's worth ruling out. Sometimes people leave breadcrumbs without realizing." Chase could almost hear Alex's mind ticking over. "Anything else out of the ordinary?"

"Not really. I mean, other than me not closing the front door properly the other day. Oh, and the power had gone out so the alarm didn't go off when the door blew open."

"What do you mean? Doesn't it have a back-up battery?"

"Um…I don't know." Obviously not. Or the battery had died and needed replacing. Shit, he'd never even thought about it. The previous owners already had the alarm system in place so all he'd done was update the security code.

"Fuck, Chase, you can't be so blasé. Remember what happened to your sister?"

"All right. Settle down. I blame ignorance regarding the alarm. But with the door, I didn't forget on purpose." In fact, his memory ninety-nine-point-nine percent reinforced he had locked up. Except, he was distracted, speaking on his mobile when he left, so he obviously hadn't. Or someone had found a way to break in and wander through his house without detection.

The thought of that sent a shit-ton of chills up his spine. Even though they hadn't taken anything, maybe they wanted to mess with him. Screw with his thinking, unnerve him, make him feel ill at ease. Send an I-can-get-to-you message.

He'd had a small amount of alcohol that night, before arriving at his place, enough not to rule out its affect. It only took one glass to impair what specifics he saw and remembered.

"I'll come by tomorrow and install the latest home-security system." Alex's tone told him not to even try to debate the issue. "You need to be more fucking careful. And I know exactly the way to ensure that." His voice had the sound-equivalent of a smug smile.

"Oh really? How?" Was he going to come around and babysit him?

"I'm assigning you protection, a personal bodyguard."

"What?" Chase jolted up, straight as a stiff, inflexible board. "No. Thank you, but not required."

"Oh yeah, it is. You just proved you're at risk. You live alone, often get home late, can't remember if you locked the door—"

"Alex."

"Chase."

"Fuck." He stabbed the speaker button, dumped his phone on the desk, and tugged on his hair, trying to restrain a growl. "I can't argue, can I? You're going to send someone, no matter what else I say."

"Yeah, I am."

He fucking knew it. Having been best buds with Alex for so long, he understood him beyond well. Knew he had no room to budge even an inch on this. "Great." Chase's voice matched his over-exaggerated eye roll. "Who should I expect?"

"I'll review my staff—their talents and availability—and get back to you."

"Fantastic. I can't wait." He tried not to let sarcasm leech through his tone. And failed.

Alex chuckled, pushing Chase's patience to the absolute maximum limit. "Me and Sage will feel a lot better knowing you're safe."

"Sage? No. Promise me you won't tell her." That's all he needed – her worrying about him as well when she had just gotten her life back in some sort of order after her own full-on ordeal.

"I have to. She's your sister and my wife. I need to protect her too. I can't have her innocently dropping by to visit you and potentially caught in a life-threatening crossfire. She's already gone through enough."

She had. And Chase didn't want to do anything that could set her back. Alex had made a valid, unarguable point. Fuck. He needed to concede. Not something he was familiar with. Rarely happened in his day job. But his day job didn't factor in the weak spots in his personal life. "Fine. So when can I likely expect my babysitter?"

Because he needed to prepare himself. He'd gotten used to a solo, do-as-I-please-as-I-want lifestyle. He'd gotten used to doing what he desired, when it suited him best, no nosy questions asked. And he wanted to keep it that way.

But a bodyguard meant full-on scrutiny. Which also threw a spanner in his free-and-easy, spontaneous sexual hook-up existence. Alex's assigned employee would need to report any new person coming and going, literally and metaphorically, from Chase's work and home. *Fuck.*

Assuming his hands weren't tied, it looked like they'd get a thorough work out for the next little while...

His office role had meant he'd never developed the hard-working calluses of a tradesman, but an extended period without the likelihood of sex suggested he might develop some self-inflicted wear and tear to his preferred palm.

"Give me a week. Hopefully less. And in the meantime, don't be last to leave work, get home before dark, and make sure all the doors and windows are locked."

"I promise I'll be extra cautious."

"Any concerns, call me. And I'll be in touch as soon as I allocate you someone."

Great.

Chapter Four

"Lexie, welcome. I'm Alex." A cool, buff, imposing man, dressed all in black — the Johnny Cash of security — greeted her in reception and directed her to his amazing office. Sunlight bathed the large room in glaring golden warmth. "Have a seat," he said, gesturing toward a comfy-looking guest chair with arms.

The big man sat behind his huge, super-neat, organized desk, eclipsing the sun, allowing her to look into his piercing blue eyes without squinting. "Thanks for giving me this opportunity."

"Thanks for coming in." Alex logged onto his computer tablet, clicked into a document and flipped through some pages. He stopped and refocused on her eyes. "So you were a police detective, injured in the line of duty."

"That's right."

"Any longstanding limitations?"

Physically, no. Psychologically... "I'm pretty much back to normal."

"Except?" He raised his eyebrows. Everything about this guy screamed don't-mess-with-me observant, in the friendliest possible way.

"I couldn't go back to my old job. They'd redeployed me but the new position didn't align with my goals." The department had taken that choice right out of her hands. "I needed a change."

After the recent discussion with her ex-boss she required a reset, to start afresh, more than ever. She couldn't ignore her drive for justice. She had to work somewhere that met that burning, inextinguishable inner urge.

He typed something into his tablet and, once again, met her gaze. "Tell me what happened. The full circumstances. Every significant detail. Not just the incident."

Oh. Shit. How much should she share? This was a job interview, not a deep and meaningful discussion with a friend. "I...why is that relevant?"

"I want to get to know you. Know what jobs to best recruit you to, if you're a successful applicant."

In other words, if she didn't open up, he'd close her down. She needed to show trust and demonstrate trustworthiness, otherwise she'd lose her chance. Either way, the result could go against her, but if she displayed a desire to participate, be honest, vulnerable, it might increase her possibility of success...if he was the type of boss who treasured those traits.

From what she'd observed so far, he'd mastered neutral body language—his eye contact, his facial expression, his tone, his posture—making his intentions, his reactions, impossible to read.

With the bills constantly coming in and her savings dwindling, she could do with a permanent, replacement job. As soon as fucking possible. In addition to the financial need, like an addict, her body craved a renewed adrenaline hit, while her mind tackled injustice. Bottom clear-as-fuck line—she required this type of role. "Can I ask you a favor?"

"You can. But I can't guarantee my help."

Fair enough, too. He'd just met her. Had no idea what she might want. Expect. Maybe she shouldn't have made the request yet, and instead given him just enough details about her previous work, her injury, and waited to see if she got the job first.

Though, from what she'd seen, if he wasn't satisfied with her responses, he'd probe. "Please don't interrupt. Please let me finish before you say anything else, ask any more questions."

His all-seeing blue eyes never left hers. "I promise." His calm steady voice and word choice correlated with his overall manner, increasing her faith in her possible future boss.

Would her willingness to follow his request, his command, to be forthcoming and honest about disclosing her past, what brought her here, increase his belief in her too?

"I...I was supposed to attend my engagement dinner, but before I left the office we got an incredible lead on a case I'd been working for months. So I couldn't ignore it and go home. I knew the situation, the players, every single person involved. I'd slogged my guts out, done a stack of overtime pulling it together, so I had to be a part of the arrest."

She averted her eyes and smoothed out her black skirt, trying to stop her leg from shaking. "I called my fiancé and told him to go ahead with our plans and I'd join the small party later. Once I was done. It should have been a simple assignment, but things didn't go to the proposed plan."

She chanced a glance at Alex, his expression interested, encouraging, but still not giving anything substantial away.

"A small team of us stood out front of a private residence, ready to enter and apprehend the assailants, when shots sounded. I hit the ground, struggling for air, pain shooting down my right arm. In absolute agony." She absentmindedly stroked the spot, the now barely visible scar a permanent reminder of the extent of her battle wounds.

"Somehow, I don't know, maybe from an adrenaline surge, I managed to chase after the fleeing group of suspects and fire my gun, putting one of them out of action before I passed out.

"I came to in hospital, doped up on pain meds but alive. Alone. I asked the nurses if my fiancé had been informed and they assured me my boss had made the call. I didn't believe it, though, because if my supposed life partner had gotten the message, why wasn't he by my side?"

The back of her eyes burned. Ridiculous. She'd cried enough for that man. She wouldn't give him the satisfaction, and she refused to break down into tears in front of the business owner, her prospective employer.

"Sore and groggy, but determined, I found my mobile shoved into one of the bedside drawers, and rang my fiancé. He didn't answer so I left a voicemail message.

"Several hours later, as I started to doze off, I heard a buzz. I checked the notifications on my phone and..." Fuck, she still couldn't quite believe what had happened. "Instead of returning my call, instead of checking how I was, the man I had planned to marry had broken up with me by text."

Lines of concern and disbelief cut through Alex's forehead. "Sorry to hear you had to go through such a horrendous experience without support. Your ex-fiancé sounds like a totally self-absorbed prick. 'Scuse my French. Fucking heartless. Did he give a reason?"

"My dedication to work, even though I'd never hidden how important it was to me. Part of him probably believed I deserved what happened because I didn't make the *right* decision. Didn't place him above my job." The more she spoke about it, the more their split felt fated. What had she seen in the guy?

Charm. The man had epitomized charisma. Always knew exactly what to say. Had shown interest, attentiveness...while it had suited his agenda.

Going by his previous dates, she wasn't his usual type. She veered toward the reserved, introverted goth side, whereas he'd preferred the stereotypical, extroverted, big-busted blondes.

So why had he chosen her? He had inherited a fuck-ton of wealth, and held a high-end, TV journalist job, so couldn't have selected her for the money. He had plenty of his own, was set up for life whether he worked or not.

What had been his driver? Some skewed idea that she might increase his social media engagement? Trying something different? A sexual appetite for variety? A compulsion to broaden his list of conquests? Compare and contrast partners so he could choose someone who met his overall narcissistic needs?

The sex had been enjoyable, she had to admit, and they'd had plenty of it, however he was and, from what she'd observed, would continue to be a massive flirt. It hadn't bothered her, though, as long as he looked, admired, appreciated, but didn't touch.

He loved women's attention, never seeming to get enough. She'd called him on it a number of times and he'd always responded with, "Don't worry. Think of it as window shopping. I'm just looking. I don't intend to handle the goods."

Don't intend to and *have no interest in* weren't quite the same. However she'd given him the benefit of the questionable doubt. Had he breached that barrier and cheated on her with another woman?

Sadly, knowing him as she did now, she wouldn't be at all shocked. Which said a lot. The whole time they'd been together he'd rarely stayed the night, and had started shouting at her, his tone and appearance frustrated and angry, on each occasion she'd gotten called into work when off duty. Particularly if he had to cancel plans he'd made.

He'd never understood or truly valued her, or the breadth of what she found important. Hence why it wouldn't have surprised her if he'd sought out comfort somewhere else to soothe the sting of what he saw as rejection.

Unlike the moon revolving around the earth, she couldn't dedicate her whole life to him alone. Romantically, yes, she could have, would have, but she also had other goals, desires, hopes, dreams. And she believed her soulmate would support her in achieving them.

So either she had a significantly flawed idea of a lifelong partner, or she hadn't yet met the right man. She hoped the answer leaned toward the latter.

"And what do you think now? Did you make the right decision?" Alex's voice cut into her troubled, mentally clogged journey into the past.

What did the *right decision* entail? Who decided what that meant? Would he judge her choice?

Didn't matter. If he didn't like what she said, it confirmed she wasn't the right fit for the role. Freed her up to find something more suitable, a job that corresponded with her thoughts and beliefs, and outlook. "I believe I did." And she'd do it again. The right man would provide support. The right man wouldn't be superficial and self-absorbed. The right man would, if not understand, empathize.

Alex propped his elbows on the desk and leaned in, as though thoroughly intrigued. "Even though you were hurt, and your engagement ended?"

It sounded harsh when he summarized it like that but he'd cut to the core of the truth. "Yes. For as long as I can remember, I've had faith in the idea that whatever is meant to be will happen. I know some people think it's airy-fairy spiritual woo-woo shit, but I reckon it's more to do with energy aligning, as well as embracing agency.

"The outcome might not necessarily take you down the path you originally envisaged, but that doesn't mean it can't be bigger and better and exactly what you need."

Alex smiled, creases forming around his intense, miss-nothing eyes. "What are your thoughts on protection work?"

Massive tangent, but still along the security, protecting-people-and-the-community route. "It interests me, it's an area I'm keen to explore."

"Do you still have a firearms license?"

"For the moment, though it's due to expire in the next few months."

"Then we need to rectify that, because you're hired. Congratulations!" Alex smiled, stood and strode around to her, wrapping her hand in a firm engulfing handshake. "I have the perfect job for you."

Chapter Five

Chase arrived at Alex's office — located in a big black skyscraper in Melbourne's central business district — and took the lift up to his mate's floor, a swarm of manic butterflies fluttering in his stomach.

Today marked the first time he'd visited his friend's new company headquarters — he just wished it was under better circumstances. He'd planned to check the place out beforehand but avoidance plus his hectic work schedule had kept him either in court or chained to his computer.

However, he could no longer ignore the persistent threats, the potential fall-out if he didn't take action. If he didn't accept Alex's offer of protection. Addressing and resolving the situation ASAP had become his crucial, stand-out, number-one priority.

He stepped into the cool, minimalist-yet-welcoming foyer, the subtle yet noticeable scent like a new-furniture showroom.

Sage sat at the sleek black reception desk, totally absorbed in whatever was on her laptop screen. "Hey, sis! What are you doing here?"

She whipped her head around and jumped up, practically glowing, a beaming smile on her face, and wrapped him in a hug. "I took some holidays to help Alexander out while he recruits to the reception position."

Chase pulled away and gave her his sternest older brother expression. Or at least that's how he hoped it looked. "That's great, but make sure you include some *you* time."

After her scary-as-fuck stalker attack, and as a way to combat compassion fatigue from her counseling role, she needed to prioritize regular self-care. She needed to allocate some time for fun.

"Oh, believe me, I have." Her cheeks flushed, giving away the ulterior motive for helping out her husband. Some afternoon delight. A definite work perk, given their intimate involvement.

Most big brothers worried about their sister falling for their best mate, but Alex was a great guy. Chase couldn't think of anyone who'd treat Sage better. Fuck, he'd helped save her life.

"Alexander didn't mention you were catching up with him for lunch." She kept the smile plastered on her lips but couldn't hide the disappointment in her eyes.

"Probably because I'm not."

"Oh?" Her curious tone had unmistakable hints of relief. "So, what are you doing he—?" Her eyes widened with sudden understanding, as though every little puzzle piece had fallen into place.

"Oh. He's worked out the best bodyguard for you. I know he had a few strong candidates. You'll be in safe hands." With a reassuring smile, she gripped his upper arms and gave them a brief squeeze.

"I hope so."

"You need to make more mindful decisions too. No more it *won't happen to me*. No more complacency. I've already made that mistake." She stared at him with a learn-from-me look. "I understand not wanting to worry anyone, thinking you're overreacting. Must run in the family."

Her brittle laugh highlighted the concern in her eyes. "If you and Alexander hadn't gotten involved when...you know, things might have worked out very differently."

They could have turned deadly.

Chase could have lost his only living relative, his beloved sister. And now the tables had flipped one-hundred-and-eighty degrees—if he didn't accept help, Sage could lose him.

Sure, she had Alex, and Chase didn't doubt his best mate would protect her over and above himself, had already shown it numerous times, but his efforts, although awesome, wouldn't replace Chase's unconditional brotherly love. Since their parents died, he and Sage had been almost inseparable.

He swallowed, trying to get a full grasp on the enormity of the existing situation. And where it could lead. Sage's words had struck home, reinforcing the importance of putting safety measures in place prior to things possibly escalating out of hand. If Alex believed a bodyguard would help, then he'd accept the guy.

As if on cue, Alex strolled into reception, gave Sage a brief kiss on the lips, then shook Chase's hand. "I'm glad you didn't wuss out."

"I said I'd come."

"You did, but knowing your resistance, I expected some urgent court matter to take precedence."

"Well, it hasn't. You'll be happy to hear I took the whole day off." Not at all easy. He'd practically had to sacrifice his first, yet-to-be-conceived child to get his leave approved at such short notice.

Alex stepped back and stared at him, lines of shock flickering in his forehead. "Who are you and what have you done with Chase?" His friend's voice dripped with sarcasm, and he and Sage struggled to stop their lips from twitching into a smirk.

Smart asses. "Hilarious. Both of you." Was there such a thing as two people being too well suited?

Alex turned to Sage and patted her ass. "Buzz me when Lexie arrives."

Lexie? Wasn't that a woman's name? Chase's already racing heart shot scarily close to heart-attack level. Surely Alex wouldn't employ a woman to protect him.

Chase darted his gaze between his sis and his best mate, but they gave nothing more away. He tugged on his T-shirt. He shouldn't overreact. Not yet. Not until he had some certainty about Lexie's specific position.

Maybe she'd applied for the receptionist role and had an interview scheduled this afternoon? Or was due to work in any one of the new number of positions? For all he knew, she'd dropped in to speak to Alex about some other case. *Fingers fucking crossed*. He didn't need some new, enthusiastic female recruit that he had to look out for on top of himself.

"Follow me." Alex led Chase into his office and *wow*. Amazing. The breathtaking space had an abundance of windows with streaming sunlight, a cool yet warm, sophisticated design — black, trimmed with gold — and on-point climate control.

He tried not to gape. He'd frequented some magnificent workplaces in Melbourne, but this made his top five. Not that he didn't expect the best from Alex — the guy was an indisputable perfectionist. He'd chosen Sage so he had to have exceptional taste.

His friend had explained he'd set himself up financially, had a great pension from the military, plus had invested successfully in the stock market, but Chase had no idea he'd done quite this well. Good on the guy. He'd worked fucking hard. Harder than hard. Put his life on the line for years to serve his country and keep citizens safe.

"You right?"

"Oh, ah, yeah." Chase stopped gawking and sat in a surprisingly comfortable seat on the opposite side of Alex's gigantic desk. "Thanks for installing the new house alarm system with battery back-up too."

"No worries. I said I would. And I don't like breaking promises. I stand by my word." Alex absolutely did. He'd shown a reliable history of it over the years.

His mate unlocked his tablet, scrolled to a page and stopped. "So, I thoroughly scanned through my list of staff, considering their interests and skills and selected someone I believe will best suit your situation."

"You didn't have to do that, but thank you."

"Yeah, I did. We already discussed it. You're my best friend and brother-in-law, and I can help."

Chase uncrossed his legs, shifted in his seat, and recrossed them the other way, nerves eating through his usual confidence. "So when will I meet my bodyguard?"

His mate moved his tablet aside and propped his forearms on his mega desk. "Any minute."

Alex's phone rang moments later, and he raised it to his ear. "Hey, babe. Excellent. Send them in." He hung up, smiled at Chase and approached the office door.

Chase swung around in his seat, eager to see the big burly don't-fuck-with-me guy Alex had chosen to look out for him. Some danger-addict dude who'd willingly put their life on the line — he didn't want or expect that, but knowing they had that mentality, plus the brute force, helped him feel more relaxed.

Holding the door open wide, his friend stepped aside and waved the person in.

A small, fair-skinned, curvaceous woman dressed all in black entered.

No. He closed his eyes, hoping that when he reopened them, the hallucination would have vanished and he'd see someone else, someone more suitable. The *real* allocated staff member.

With great consternation, he cracked open his eyelids.

No. Not her. He shook his head as though to shake the incongruent image from his mind. But the same woman stood there, staring at him with large, unblinking eyes, one dark eyebrow cocked. By the quizzical look on her face, she'd already pegged him as some judgmental, misogynistic prick.

The cute, impish little goth couldn't be his assigned agent. So who the fuck was she? And where was his big, buff, strapping bodyguard?

Alex closed the door, ushered the woman to a seat beside Chase and returned to his throne. "Chase, this is Lexie. She'll be working closely with you until we find who's sending the threats and if they're a serious concern."

Chase glared at his best mate. "Lexie is a female."

"Yeah. You really are very observant." Alex didn't even try to hide his sarcastic grin.

"Um, hello? I can hear you, you know. And I can even comprehend what you're saying." A sardonic yet sultry feminine voice caressed his ears.

Chase darted his gaze to her. If words could slay someone, then yes, she'd be a brilliant choice for his bodyguard. But they didn't. He needed a person packed with physical power, with bucketloads of brawn and endurance. Whereas she looked like she'd struggle to swat a fly let alone protect him under dire, deadly circumstances. Fuck. How had Alex chosen *her*? How had he decided she'd best fit the role?

Either he was scarily short on staff or didn't see anywhere near what Chase saw — the restrictions, the limitations, the sexy, spirited, petite little unsuitable specimen. His brow puckered with disbelief. "You're *not* my minder."

"Actually, I am." Her potent stare challenged his response, the green in her slate eyes flaring.

Chase spluttered and shot an incredulous stare at Alex, throwing his hands out as if to say, *what the fuck? You can't be serious.*

"She's the most qualified person for the job. She'll be a tremendous asset. You won't have to worry about a thing."

How could his best friend not assess her the same way? How could he sound so bloody calm and confident?

"Says who?" Fuck, how could *she* keep him safe? He wanted to wrap her in a hug, and maybe see where things led...

"Me." With those two little letters, that one short word, her tone had resounded with absolute strength and sureness.

Beyond unexpected, and kind of hot. He fixed his eyes on her, testing to see if she would wilt under the added pressure.

"Your stereotypical reaction and assumption has been the key to my success. People, *men*, don't expect much from a woman of small stature. And that's their biggest mistake."

The potency of her gaze suggested she didn't back down easy, and reinforced her stance—she'd gotten accustomed to guys fobbing her off, and she wouldn't put up with their unsubstantiated views, their limited, prejudicial shit.

Suddenly, he didn't want to face her in a dark, deserted alley. Hopefully he wouldn't have to. Unless it was for something more...enjoyable. She had a professional, no-bullshit edge to her eyes that added to her appeal. However, he couldn't and wouldn't act on that.

Yeah, he'd describe her as attractive, in her own unique way, but she wasn't his regular type. Plus she'd agreed to be his bodyguard, so they'd soon sign a binding, professional contract. And from her reaction to him so far, she'd knee his balls into his throat if he even attempted to make a move.

Chase flashed her his signature, charismatic smile. The one that melted the frostiest woman. Usually. "Can't wait to work with you."

"Don't fuck with me. Just stick with your honesty. It's best for both of us if we're clear on where we stand. No polite-but-fake bullshit, and no come ons, no trying to get any extra benefits. I'm here to do a job and I'd appreciate it if you don't cause any extra difficulties." Her glare alone could have frozen his cock off.

Fuck me.

Scary, yet intriguing. Made him want to win her over. He'd always seen someone's negativity as a challenge. Always worked extra hard to get them over the positive invisible line. And when he did, fuck it was rewarding. Made his day that much brighter.

She'd probably intended the controlled venom in her voice to put him in his place, turn him off. But bizarrely, her take-charge, confident attitude turned him on. Not that he'd let her know…yet. Maybe never.

For now, he'd trust Alex's assessment and let her attempt to provide protection. But the second he felt unsafe, he'd feedback his concerns to his best mate. And tell her last, unless he wanted to kiss his family jewels goodbye.

"So glad this meeting went well." Chase couldn't miss Alex's signature smirk.

His friend might be having a bit of fun with him but he had to keep reminding himself that Alex wouldn't have done anything to put him in jeopardy, he wouldn't have appointed a dud, wouldn't have chosen someone he couldn't trust to do the required job. So no matter Chase's reluctance, he had to go with the guy's expert choice. He had to trust him, like he had with his own sister's life.

Chase met Alex's gaze. "So what's the plan from here?"

"Lexie will follow you home and remain stationed across the street."

Right across the fucking street? He didn't require that level of surveillance. "What? No. I'm fine. I don't need someone watching my every move."

"Something to hide?" Lexie raised her eyebrows, a smart-ass smile on her Hollywood-starlet-like face. She'd thrown down the proverbial gauntlet and no way would he give her the satisfaction of surrender.

He swallowed, not at all used to that sort of challenging response from women. Most of them fawned all over him. "No." Except he didn't want judgment about his lifestyle.

He liked a no-strings-attached fuck or two, with different partners, and what was wrong with that? He was safe, responsible. Always used a condom, got tested regularly. Always remained upfront about wanting something casual, mostly one-off.

Always made sure his hook-ups understood and agreed to the terms. So it shouldn't matter what Lexie thought, what anyone else thought. But it did. He preferred his private life to remain private.

"Great. Lexie, I'll text you the details of the Airbnb I've booked you into, directly across from Chase's place. Once you're checked in, watch for anything unusual and let me know any updates. Doesn't matter what time."

"You can count on me." Something about her confident, husky voice spoke right to Chase's cock.

He subtly shook his head in a feeble attempt to shake her from his system. Could he count on her? When it came down to external appearance, Lexie didn't look like she could harm a bug, except through her hard-as-fuck, slicing stare and carefully chosen cutting words.

And maybe the occasional well-timed knee to the balls. But none of those would stop a determined offender set on vengeance.

Alex locked on Chase's eyes with a don't-fuck-this-up stare. "Go about your daily routine. Behave as though you're following through on your usual schedule. In other words, we want this person to think everything is normal. The second they suspect the slightest change, we're fucked. You even more so. We want to get this guy...or woman. We don't want to scare them off and leave the threat lingering. Got it?"

"Got it." Chase held back the compulsion to salute. Alex was helping him—he didn't need Chase's retaliatory, childish, sulky response. Fucking him off would be totally stupid and ungrateful.

The time to fuck around had gone. Whether he wanted to believe it or not, things had gotten super serious. And he was too young, and had too many goals and aspirations to die.

* * * *

Lexie got into her car and followed Chase back to his house. What the fuck was wrong with the guy? Yes, okay, with his Chris Hemsworth vibe she could see the outward attraction. See how women may overlook some of his faults. But how did they ignore the man's stubborn, arrogant attitude? She couldn't. It was a massive turn off. It didn't help that he had *player* written all over him.

She'd been there, thoroughly done that. Never again. Her charming ex had done more than a total number on her, but she'd learned this time. A man could use the prettiest words in the world but if he didn't back them with action it meant fuck all. Purely, one-hundred-and-fifty percent lip service.

When it came to serious shit, the life-threatening crunch, how would the person react? Would they be reliable or willing to break up because they didn't get their way, their self-absorbed needs met, or would they view the situation with a broader perspective?

She needed a broader-perspective-type guy.

Stop it.

It didn't fucking matter right now. Work required her full focus. Chase was a job, not her date. He didn't even fall into the realm of dateable material. Hook-up, yeah. Given his undeniable sex appeal, she'd possibly make an exception to her recent no one-night-stand rule and consider him for a few hours of physical fun — as long as he kept his mouth shut, and they weren't working together professionally.

Otherwise, forget it. Any poor woman who fell for the guy beyond a short-term affair would be fucked. Literally and figuratively.

Lexie could deal with his bullshit for work. In fact, she should be grateful. He'd provided an opportunity to prove her worth, her value to herself, to Solve Security. However, she wouldn't admit her appreciation. Not aloud. The guy already had a gigantic enough head he could barely fit through the door.

Chase pulled into some fancy property with flashy, ornate iron gates, opened by remote, of course, and a ridiculously long, tree-lined driveway. It wouldn't surprise her if he had *staff* too. A butler, cook, cleaner, gardener, personal assistant. Someone to wipe his smart ass.

Lexie parked in the Airbnb across the road, and wrenched up the handbrake. She drew in a deep breath and unclenched her teeth. This man would be the metaphorical, if not literal death of her. His personality already grated on her nerves and she'd only met him for a few minutes.

At least she didn't have to stay in the same residence. Babysitting a self-absorbed lothario, and having to watch him do his thing, didn't exactly float her rocking boat. But she'd do what she needed to do...within reason. Chase was her boss's best mate — more motivation for why she couldn't afford to fuck this up.

She checked into the cute little self-contained cottage, a couple weeks' worth of clothes and toiletries, her trusty, high-powered, whisper-quiet panty vibrator and her phone and laptop chargers, already packed in advance, in preparation for, well, anything.

Next, she focused on getting sorted for the evening. She had enough resources with her to stick things out in the short term. If she remained at the same location, with access to a supermarket, and washing machine or laundromat. Hopefully the whole situation would be a false alarm and get resolved within the week, max. If not, she'd drop by her place and replenish her supplies the second she got the chance.

As soon as she grabbed a towel and got naked, ready for a shower, her phone rang. So bloody typical.

She whipped her mobile out of her handbag, in case it was Alex — Chase. Impeccable timing. It was like he had a camera in her place or some filthy sixth sense. She assumed it was the latter.

Lexie stared at the screen, her forehead crinkled. What could he want? She debated whether to let it go to voicemail, but she couldn't ignore her client's call. She had to respond. He could be in trouble.

She swiped to answer and hit speaker. "Yeah?"

"Hello to you, too." She could hear the smart-ass smirk in his velvety voice. "All settled in?"

"What's the problem?"

"No problem."

"Then why did you call?"

"I wanted to see if you'd eaten dinner. If not, I make a mean spaghetti and meatballs. You're welcome to join me."

Her mouth watered. How long had it been since she'd had a home-cooked meal? Months. Since before the accident. Restaurant home-delivery services had been a life saver. But she missed that personal touch.

Cooking for one had never appealed, especially once her fiancé had broken things off. And yet, she couldn't go there, increase the connection with her client. Because no matter what someone said or thought, eating together equaled intimacy. "No thanks."

"Are you sure? There's plenty. And not to sound arrogant, but the sauce tastes amazing."

Him? Not sound arrogant? Hilarious. She almost burst out laughing. He couldn't not sound arrogant if he tried. "No, I'm fine. Thank you." Except she wasn't. She licked her lips and swallowed the flood of saliva in her mouth. She hadn't gotten around to organizing dinner yet. And his offer sounded way too tempting.

"Your loss. If you change your mind, let me know. Otherwise, I'll see you tomorrow. Sweet dreams."

Before she could respond, he'd hung up.

Sweet dreams. She wished. She hadn't had any of those for a very long time.

Chapter Six

The house alarm went off, yanking Chase from a fantastic dream. A sexy, petite Lexie-like woman with long black hair and stunning eyes was just about to blow him. He wanted to go back to sleep and see it through to the climactic end, but he couldn't ignore the noise.

He rubbed his bleary eyes, jumped out of bed, threw on some boxers then, mobile phone in hand, raced to silence the replacement state-of-the-art alarm system Alex had recently installed.

Chase switched it off, then scanned downstairs to see what had tripped the sensors. It didn't take long to find the problem.

In the lounge room, someone had thrown a large rock through the bay window, shattering the glass all over the window seat and carpet. He bent down to have a closer look at a white envelope wrapped around the jagged stone but refrained from touching it. Hard to do when curiosity, like an insistent itch, drove him to find out what the note said.

Chase continued through the house, noticing no other breaches, and let his home security service know, then sat on a glass-free couch and called Alex.

"What's wrong?" His friend sounded groggy, like he'd woken him up from a deep sleep. Chase glanced at the time. *Fuck*. Only five-thirty a.m.

"Sorry, mate. Ah...someone threw a rock through my window and it has a letter attached."

"Don't touch it." Alex suddenly sounded wide awake.

"I haven't."

"Good. Have you told Lexie?"

"Not yet."

"Do that, then get ready and come to my office."

But he was supposed to go into work today. Business as bloody usual, or so Alex had rammed home. "Why?" Chase spoke into dead air. Alex had already ended the call.

Chase speed-dialed Lexie's number and scrubbed his scruff with his free hand. "Good morning."

"Fuck, Chase."

He wished. Going by the short amount of time he'd spent with her, the little he knew, she came across as though she'd be a wild woman, a total spitfire in bed. His favorite sort of hook up. Except she was off limits. And she showed not one ounce of interest in him, not even a skerrick of attraction.

Her grumpy-as-fuck voice suggested she didn't mean the words quite in the way he'd fantasized. More like *fuck off, Chase*.

"Sorry to disturb your beauty sleep but Alex asked me to call you."

"Why didn't he phone me himself?"

"Because I need to show you something at my place."

"Really? Let me guess — that's your most successful pick-up line. Well, you know what? That shit doesn't, and never will, work on me. Understand?"

Hmmm…the lady doth protest overly much. But he'd explore that further later. "It's in my top three but no, that's not why I called. Someone threw a rock through my lounge room window with an envelope taped to it. Alex wanted you to come and check it out, and then for us to meet him in his office."

"Meet in his office? What for?"

"To bag the evidence and show him? To give it to forensics to process? To go through my version and your assessment of the fucking mess? I don't fucking know. He hung up before I could get more details. I figured we'd find out soon enough."

"Fine. I'll see you shortly. Lock yourself in a room and I'll call when I get there."

"All right." Did she think someone might be hiding inside somewhere, ready to jump him? He'd been so busy trying to address the blaring alarm and phoning the required people he hadn't even considered that the perp might have entered his house and hidden, waiting to attack.

The idea freaked him out, but she could be right. He strode to his downstairs bathroom and secured the bolt on the door. "Done."

She paused and he almost disconnected the call. "Oh, are you okay?"

"Yeah. Thanks for asking. See you soon." Definitely not an early-morning person but props to her for pushing past the obvious inconvenience to check on his wellbeing.

Chase had an express shower and wrapped a towel around his waist. The moment she arrived, he'd get to work on a batch of scones — half cheese, half plain. And he had salted butter, thickened cream and strawberry jam in the fridge. He had a gnawing feeling in his gut that they'd need plenty of sustenance today.

Would she select sweet or savory? Or maybe a mixture? If he went with his instinct, he'd pick her as a savory girl, a cheese-platter-and-red-wine-over-dessert type. He couldn't wait to see if he'd assessed her correctly. Going by his elite observational skills and resulting high number of career wins, and lady conquests, he was rarely wrong.

* * * *

Twenty-three minutes later, Lexie entered the pedestrian side gate at Chase's place, just as tall and imposing as the main entrance, but without a check-in point, without any way to alert him that someone had entered the property.

Much too easily accessible. Maybe he'd thought the house alarm security system was enough? No one could ever be too careful. Especially not in his line of work. She'd make a note to mention it to Alex, now that the culprit had made a more concerning statement.

She followed the path through a stunning garden, surrounded by tall trees and colorful native plants, arriving at his equally impressive front door six minutes later. Not as efficient as she'd prefer but still reasonable, still better than too late. She had little tolerance for tardiness, and even less for broken promises.

Lexie called his number and waited, the broken front window catching her attention. Obviously the assailant had scoped out the area, approached on foot in the dark and escaped through the garden. Concealed. Unseen. Unheard, except for the broken glass and alarm going off.

After several rings he answered, and before he could utter a word she said, "I'm at the front." And hung up.

In less than twenty seconds, the door whooshed open, revealing Chase—hair wet, unshaven—wearing only a towel that barely covered his crown jewels and thoroughly exposed his muscular chest.

She tried not to lick her lips. Okay, he was hot. And she had the emotional maturity to admit it. To herself. Didn't mean anything other than an appreciation of male beauty. He could be the most gorgeous man alive but it meant nothing if he was a dick. Chase had annoying tendencies, but he hadn't behaved like a prick yet, according to her personal criteria. However, he had potential, given his overt lack of faith in her protective capabilities.

"Nice and quick, as promised."

The opposite of how she liked sex. So not relevant to the current situation. Lexie wrangled her mind back into the moment and stared him in the eye. "I told you, you can count on me. I'm true to my word."

"You are. Come on in." He waved her inside, that signature sexy smile of his crinkling the corners of his too-observant eyes.

Did he burn those aromatic candles that smelled like mouthwatering sin?

"Let me get dressed and I'll start on breakfast while you look around."

Did he have to get dressed? Damn.

No. Better for both of them. "You don't have to make anything."

"I want to. How many times can you eat fast food muffins?"

A lot, going by her experience. But fine. If he wanted to go to that trouble, let him. Obviously, he wasn't deterred by her rejection of his dinner invite last night. "Well, get to it. We can't muck around." She couldn't afford to fuck off her boss on her first job.

Her stomach growled even though her normal routine consisted of a take-away coffee and brunch, only eating early in the morning when on holidays. And this was far from a holiday.

While she stood there, trying not to gawk, he slipped past her, and practically sprinted up the stairs, the towel hugging his taut butt.

She blew out a built-up breath and entered a large room on the left, appreciating its full grandeur. Intricate, decorative cornices, a real fireplace with a fantastic marble mantelpiece, and buttery chocolate leather couches that she'd love to sink into. He had money and he made the most of it. Didn't even try to hide his wealth. Not that there were any rules to say he should.

Shards of glass from the broken bay window had scattered over the window seat and shiny timber floor. The untouched rock, so harmless now, sat immobile, yet its sharp edges had scratched and scraped the wood where it had crashed and rolled before stopping dead.

Lexie grabbed her phone out of her cavernous handbag and took photos of the scene, then did a thorough sweep of his house, leaving his bedroom until last.

She knocked on the door. "You decent?"

"Never." His rich, deep, raspy laugh penetrated the door.

She should have expected that comeback. He had a reputation as a fast-thinking, quick-witted man. An articulate charmer with a renowned smart mouth.

"Come on in," he said, his tone totally devilish.

With a shaky hand she gripped the handle and entered to find him standing by the wardrobe tucking himself into snug khaki cargo pants, a fitted white shirt stretching across his broad chest.

Damn him for being so delectable. She glanced away and focused on ensuring the space was safe, searching his balcony and en suite. When she returned to his bedroom, he'd gone.

One last check of the upper floor revealed no signs of a break-in or highlighted any spots for an intruder to hide. Relieved, she descended the grand, windy internal staircase and found him in the kitchen, off the living room, making…something.

Before visiting his home, she'd expected cold, ultra-modern, minimalist décor, a house with no real character, but the interior radiated a surprisingly welcome warmth. Honey-toned timber floors stretched down the corridor, and extended into the large, open-plan living area.

"The scones will be ready soon. Hope you're hungry."

She whipped her head up, his piercing eyes fixing on hers. Rolling the bowl of mixture into balls, he placed them on a greased tray.

A surge of saliva filled her mouth. She hoped she wouldn't dribble when she spoke. She hadn't had homemade scones since her grandmother was alive ten plus years ago. "Thanks. I'll just finish this." Lexie studied the living room in greater detail, taking extra macro photos and videos of the mess with her phone to show Alex.

In what felt like only a few minutes, Chase placed a couple of plates of scones and small bowls of condiments on the breakfast bar. "Come and have some before they get cold." He smiled and pulled out a bar stool.

She swallowed, and focused on him with her firmest stare. "Um...I believe I'm the person in charge here. I call the required shots, have the final say on our schedule."

"I'm not disputing that. But you still need to eat. Helps brain function, as I'm sure you know. Might assist you to see more, make more sense of the scene."

She clamped her teeth together. He might have a point but fuck if she'd give him the satisfaction of admitting it. Lexie fought against the impulse to shake her head. This guy would cause her no end of trouble. "Don't you want to know what the letter says?"

"Yeah. But whether we open it now or in half an hour, nothing will have changed. It'll still have the same content. And to be honest, I'd rather hold off and enjoy my breakfast. Given the delivery method, I'd bet my life it's not a positive message. Somehow, I don't think it's an invitation or to announce I've come into a shit-ton of money. Do you?" Chase raised his eyebrows in question, and kept his hold on the back of the bar stool.

Like he didn't already have a shit-ton of money. But, anyway, she couldn't argue. And he knew. He'd made a strong, impossible-to-contest point. His specialty. She dropped her phone into her bag and approached him, his I-gotcha smile kicking up the corners of his smug lips.

She sat and couldn't help but inhale the delicious savory aroma. *Cheese scones. No way.* She loved cheese so damn much. How could he have known? Or maybe he liked it too? Oh yeah, she could see him with the fancy, overpriced wine and preposterously expensive cheese platter.

Going by what he'd laid out, he'd made a mixed batch—there were plain scones as well, with a dish of butter, one of strawberry jam and another of thickened cream. Lexie loved a Devonshire Tea too. It had to be a coincidence. It's not like Alex had included a favorite-foods questionnaire as part of her application.

"What are you waiting for?" He held out a set of tongs. "Have some. As you can see, there's plenty. I made more than enough for both of us. I figured we'd need the energy."

Why did that sound so flirtatious, so sexually insinuating? She had to be reading into things. Big time. It had to reflect her thinking, like an auditory version of an inkblot test. Showed the inner workings of her mind whether she was ready to deal with them or not.

Why had her brain even deviated down that track? She had to have masochistic tendencies, because from what she'd seen and learned about him, she was the opposite of his type.

But then again, her internet deep-dive into all things Chase last night—for work purposes—confirmed he was a well-known womanizer, so maybe he didn't have particularly strict selection criteria.

She didn't think it in a self-derogatory way, more just acknowledging the fact that he found a wide range of females attractive. Most likely any available, semi-decent woman craving sex. With him.

Well, guess what? Even if he begged, no matter how handsome his outer appearance, she'd take great pleasure in refusing. Refusing to be one of his devout, fan-girl minions.

Her stomach gurgled again. Persistent. Snitch. She took the tongs from his outstretched hand. "Thank you."

After less than a moment's deliberation, she selected a cheese and a plain scone. Might as well try both, seeing as he'd gone to such an effort. And she'd hate to see food wasted. She had a history of trying each option in her personal life too, couldn't stand seeing opportunities thrown away. She laughed to herself. Little did he know, or would ever find out. Only those close to her won that privilege.

Lexie avoided further eye contact, determined not to pander to his ego-centric personality. She'd been burned by guys like that in the past, Chase's similar traits ringing deafening alarm bells.

She sliced her still-steaming cheese scone in half and slathered a bit of butter onto each side. It melted into the fluffy center, making her mouth water. One bite into the crispy, golden top piece, and she moaned. Like uninhibited, ultimate orgasm stuff. In fact, she couldn't remember ever sounding so overtaken with pleasure from well, anything.

Quickly swallowing the delicious morsel in her mouth, she tried to discreetly glance at Chase. Of course he stared right back, super proud, extra conceited. Maybe he did meet her pompous-dick criteria.

"Sounds like you're glad you tried it."

Another innuendo-infused statement. "I am. It really hit the spot." *Step right up, mister.* She could play that game too, and beat the best of them.

"Good to hear. That's my aim—to always hit the perfect spot with everything I do." He carefully pried open a plain scone, spread a sliver of strawberry jam onto each portion then spooned on some cream. Next he bit into one half and licked off the remnants from his lips in the most erotic way imaginable. Or at least, that's how it looked.

Had he meant it? He had to have done it on purpose. She squeezed her legs together and hoped like hell he didn't notice. He'd probably planned to get a reaction out of her, and he had. But fingers crossed she'd kept her response subtle.

Lexie finished her cheese scone and focused on her plate, while he told her all about his stand-out past prosecutor stories. Did he enjoy talking about himself, hearing the sound of his own radio-quality voice, or had he hoped to engage her, encourage renewed eye contact, provide her with extra, possibly useful information?

Whatever his aim, it had a massive side benefit—she didn't have to worry about filling the conversational space. Being a full-on introvert, speaking incessantly was far from her forte. Unless it was a topic she loved—social justice, cats, all things black.

Thankfully, he could talk enough crap to easily cover both of them, from what she'd witnessed. Okay, not exactly crap. She'd never admit it to him but what he'd said had held her interest. So unusual, because she had a notoriously short attention span for those who chatted nonstop. However, he had a natural, engrossing story-telling ability.

She sliced open her plain scone, spread a generous serve of strawberry jam — because although she loved cheese, she couldn't deny she also had a sugar addiction — and scooped on a decent dollop of cream.

Lexie bit into the bottom half of her scone and couldn't stop her groan of appreciation. *Noooo!* Not again! This man already had the fattest head ever. She knew she shouldn't have succumbed to his request to taste his food.

The guy would only ever suggest something he excelled at to stroke his ego, to meet his insecurity issues. And she had to keep that in mind. Yes, he could talk, cook, act considerate, but that didn't redeem him for cocky, player-like behavior.

Stop it. Stop. It. She was not in a relationship with Chase and never would be, so why give a fuck who he slept with, whether he was or wasn't a player, unless it impacted on the investigation. Right. *Right?*

"What do you think?"

You're a presumptuous, self-absorbed, needy guy, with culinary skills and pretty-boy looks requiring unconditional support. And fanfare. A fuck-ton of fan-girl fanfare. But she couldn't say that to his face. "Thanks for breakfast."

He flashed her his signature, Simon the Likeable, or in this case, Chase the Likeable smile. Somewhat sexy, somewhat roguish, somewhat annoying. "My pleasure."

Enough about him and his narcissistic need for flattery. She had to safely and meticulously finish processing the scene before checking in with Alex. "Do you have gloves?" She normally carried a stash but in her hurry, had left them in her car.

"Yeah. Who doesn't these days. I'll grab some," he said, and left the room.

A couple of minutes later, he returned and handed her a box of the latex-free variety. "Go for it."

She hand sanitized, snapped a pair into place and met his gaze. "Do you have any Ziploc bags? Something that will fit this rock?"

"I do." He took off into the kitchen, yanked open a cupboard and, in under a minute, returned with a handful.

She carefully peeled off the envelope, and lifted the now bare rock into one of the bags. *Hopefully not free from fingerprints or any other DNA.* Then she pried open the sticky envelope seal and extracted the note. "Ready?" She tried not to shake, but she couldn't control the adrenaline coursing through her body.

Chase crowded in close to her, the scent of his clean, fresh, woodsy cologne spiking her senses. "What does it say?"

She unfolded the letter and read it word for exact word. *"You need to let Mike go. Now. If you don't, watch out."*

"Mike DeSalvo, fuck. I knew it." He shoved his hands through his still-damp hair and huffed out a stressed-sounding breath.

"Your most recent conviction." The long-sought-after, finally caught — *thank fuck* — serial rapist?

"Yeah." He ran his palms over his face and struggled to stand still.

She wanted to grab his forearm to hold him steady, to ground him, but refrained. Too intimate. She had to focus on her role, retain some distance. So instead, she bagged the envelope and letter in another Ziploc. "Tell me, who is willing to put you in danger, themselves at risk, to get Mike released?" Who on earth wanted someone like that back on the streets terrorizing women, society?

He met her questioning gaze, his forehead creased. "I don't know. From what I was told, based on our department's restricted-budget research, he didn't have any close family or friends. Definitely not anyone who'd go to this extent."

Whoever had chosen this path had to be just as crazy, just as screwed. "Okay. Let's gather everything up, present it to Alex and see what he says."

Chapter Seven

Alex greeted him and Lexie at the reception desk, ushered them into his office, without a word, and shut the door, his facial expression stony as fuck. "You need to go to your country cabin."

What? "Where's Sage?"

"Getting pampered. I booked her a few days at a spa down the coast."

Safe. "Good." The further she stayed away from him, the better for the moment. Alex must have thought similarly, even with limited information about the most recent developments. The rock. The envelope. The note.

Chase and Lexie had told him vaguely about it, and had handled everything with gloves so as not to contaminate any of the articles with their own fingerprints, their own DNA. They'd stored and transported the raw items securely, and carried the Ziploc bags with them in order to lodge the objects for thorough processing.

Maybe the assailant had gotten lazy, fucked up. Chase had worked enough cases to know that most offenders weren't master criminals. Most would get caught eventually. Often from the simplest, smallest thing they'd overlooked. The lab needed to do all the tests. The advances in DNA technology in particular, had helped heaps. Assuming without facts, without data, meant nothing.

"Did you hear what I said?"

Chase pressed his palms onto Alex's pristine desktop. "What happened to behaving normally? Isn't leaving town a bit extreme, a bit premature?"

His best mate's gaze fixed on Chase's aggressive posture, his hands fucking up the shiny surface. "No. I should have sent you there straight away. I'd hoped the situation would blow over but it's escalated. And I need you both to be as safe and as hard to find as possible. Until this whole thing is resolved."

Maybe it was Alex's natural being or military training, or both, but he had this innate, clear, almost soothing-but-don't-fuck-with-me calm. Perfect for the leader of his new protection and security business.

"While you're away, I'll get your window sorted, and heighten the security of any additional access points into your property. Then I'll investigate every avenue, as subtly and thoroughly as possible."

Without question, he knew Alex would do exactly what he promised. Chase had known his mate for more than half his life and he trusted him and his expertise implicitly.

"And what do you need from me?" Lexie's sexy voice broke their bro-bond.

Chase turned his head right as she stepped forward, her tight black tank top clinging to her torso and her slim-fit jeans conforming to her legs. She didn't even afford him a glance, staring Alex straight in the eye.

"Watch him. Don't let him out of your sight. Not for a minute...unless directed. And bring your phone and laptop and chargers because I'll send you updates as soon as information becomes available. And I expect you to keep me posted with what's happening on your end."

"For sure. I promised I wouldn't let you down and I won't." Lexie stepped back, leaving Chase facing off against his best friend. A best friend that cared about him and would do anything to save his life. Probably risk his own. He had for Sage, for his military mates, for his country. And he'd do it again. And again. And again. Whatever it took.

Resistance stabbed at his stomach, however he had no choice but to go along with the plan. Chase pushed off the desk, leaving sweaty, mottled handprints. "We'll head home, pack, then get going."

Alex glanced at the smeared palm prints and back at Chase. He'd mastered a neutral, poker-faced expression, but Chase knew imperfections grated the guy's gears. "Let me know when you arrive."

As soon as they left, he expected Alex to come out with a cloth to clean up the oily marks messing with the sheen of his desk. It almost made him laugh. He wished he could capture it on camera as evidence to give his buddy a hard time...and Chase would, once he escaped his own huge mess.

He and Lexie drove back to her place to collect some more clothes and toiletries, then headed to his, in contemplative silence. Well, it was for him. Working through what had happened, the latest developments, where to from this point. But then he planned to talk through options, strategies.

How much could he say to her? How much could he trust the guarded woman? He hadn't known her long enough to read all her telltale behaviors. He still couldn't believe she hadn't commented on his car. The first woman ever to not give a fuck.

Taking the back, tree-lined suburban streets, he hoped to avoid anyone tailing him and reach his house in good time. He hoped she'd eventually say something, clue him into her thinking. But so far — not a word.

Had she zoned out? Did she need time to absorb the info and process it? He'd love to pick her unbiased brain, discuss her professional opinion, background and recommendations. Sooner rather than too-late later. Though, he couldn't force it.

Everyone had their own way of dealing with things. But he would eventually work out her preferred patterns of conduct. And what they meant. Over a number of years in his profession, he'd honed that skill.

If a lawyer wanted results, he relied heavily on people-reading. But in this instance, he had less leeway, less luxury to wait too long, he needed to get a workable answer in half the 'normal' time.

Although he embodied the legal version of a psychologist, he had a more skewed agenda. Like advertisers, they had to excel at picking apart people's psyches, what drove their decision making, to know how to best pitch to them and obtain the desired outcome.

So if he and Lexie were forced together long enough, which could very well be the case, he believed in his ability to get a handle on what made her tick. And hopefully tap into the answers he required.

Chase parked in the driveway and turned to her. "Meet me back here in an hour?"

"No. You heard Alex. I need to stay with you. Then once you're done, we'll detour past the accommodation and I'll check out and load all my stuff into your car.

How much luggage would he have to accommodate? He shoved a hand through his hair and breathed out hard, but didn't argue. Instead, he focused on the practicalities, and did as she asked.

After he packed his cases, and filled an insulated container with edible leftovers and bags of ice, he carried them down the corridor toward the front door. She stood in the main hallway, looking as fresh and perfect as he did for court, her shiny black hair slicked back, not a strand out of place, and wound into a bun at the base of her head. Had she freshened up in his downstairs bathroom? She must have.

Every single time they'd met, no matter the hour, she'd worn that immaculate hairstyle. He itched to let her locks loose, so they flowed across her back and shoulders. How he'd love to run his fingers through her lustrous long hair.

Not possible. Incredibly inappropriate in the current circumstances. Yeah, he needed a pleasant distraction but he also had to remember she had a protection job to do, while they both kept their minds on their environment, discerning any possible perps, on staying out of danger.

From what he'd observed, she always stuck to the designated timeframe, had never been late, which worked well for him because he couldn't tolerate excuses. He'd always equated it with laziness, selfishness, unprofessionalism, lack of drive, lack of caring.

That sounded harsh. He had some flexibility. He understood sometimes things happened that were beyond a person's control. But mostly, in his experience, they occurred infrequently.

They loaded his car, then detoured past the Airbnb. Somehow, she fit her sports bag inside a single suitcase squeezing it in beside his two pieces of luggage, plus the food-filled Esky. He couldn't believe she'd packed lighter than him. He'd never dated a woman who traveled with fewer bags. Ever. *Fucking intriguing.* Everything about her had him mystified.

And he had to fucking stop his fascination. She had been hired to keep him safe. Though, for all her apparent expertise, he didn't see how. He could practically bench press her one handed.

Okay, yes, he didn't know the extent of her work history and he relied on her to tell him — because she needed to disclose those sorts of details — not Alex. But he couldn't force her. Even if she had an exemplary record of security work, it probably wasn't enough to shut down his inner drive to protect her, protect both of them.

He didn't want to die but he also strove to keep his conscious clear by making sure she didn't become entangled within the crosshairs of his fucking predicament. A shitstorm of his own creation. But the facts were, she'd placed herself within his intricate, dangerous web. He hadn't asked her for help. Alex had thrust her professional assistance upon him.

For most of the trip up the mind-numbing, repetitive, paddock-filled highway, she remained glued to her smartphone, either talking on it, replying to emails and messages or typing notes.

Kind of frustrating, because he'd had his brief reflection period but now he'd like to talk. Generally he loved conversation. It assisted with his stress management and enhanced his connections with others. It also helped him stay alert when driving long distances.

After practically wearing out his peripheral vision, Chase turned onto a scenic road, one of the prettiest parts of the drive—showcasing a smattering of sumptuous wineries, rocky outcrops, and sections with some tall and uniquely gnarled, knotted trees—and glanced at Lexie, her focus still trained on her mobile. "Have you been to high country Victoria before?"

She snapped her head up, as though awoken from a Sleeping-Beauty-style slumber. "No," she said, her tone short, her gaze immediately returning to her phone. Totally missing the magnificence of the area. Such a shame. Such a waste. But obviously it wasn't her jam.

He was a job, a money-making enterprise. A fucking life-threatening one, but cash-filled all the same. And she had willingly decided to take the chance.

"Do you like nature?"

She didn't even look up this time. "I believe in saving the environment."

"That doesn't really answer my question." He glanced at her and she shrugged. "You don't like speaking much, do you?"

She shot him a stare that said, *wow, you finally worked it out.* "What made you come to that conclusion?" Sarcasm dripped from every word, like sticky, viscous honey.

Bloody hell. He'd be sharing a small space with the woman of few sarcastic phrases for who knew how long. They had opposite communication styles and her responses rammed home that she didn't view him in a particularly positive light, pointing toward a strained, combative few days. Possibly weeks, months.

Fuck. Their current trajectory showed a terribly bumpy ride. Maybe he should have just risked it with his assailant.

The negative forecast predicted they'd either drive each other nuts or kill one another before the guy — or girl — got anywhere near them. Though, from his years of experience, the perpetrator's writing style and use of language suggested a man. Didn't mean he'd gotten it right, but he gave himself a ninety-five percent accuracy rate.

Lexie returned to her phone, while he refocused on the road, getting them to the local shops safely. He desperately needed a strong coffee, and they required at least a fortnight's worth of food. The less they entered into town and made physical contact with others, the safer for everyone. "We have to grab some groceries before we continue to the cabin."

Several lines of frustration puckered her forehead. "Can't you order online like almost everyone else these days?"

"The cupboards are pretty bare and the fridge is empty, so no. We need some basics. Plus, I like to pick my own meat and fresh fruit and veggies. So let's load up now and order online after, okay? I promise we'll only stop briefly. My place is up the mountain, which isn't too far. We'll be done before you know it. Hardly anyone will even notice we're here."

"What's not too far?"

"Forty-five minutes or so, depending on traffic and weather conditions."

She rolled her eyes. "Great. And how many people know where your cabin's located?"

Shit. A few. "A handful, but they have no idea when I'm visiting. I have no set vacation times. No one will suspect I'm around, unless they see me."

"So stay in the shadows."

"Like the Phantom. I get it." His favorite superhero. "I plan to slip in and out, while you stay on your phone. I know the layout of the supermarket. I know where to find everything. So I'll get what we need in no time." He reached for the car door handle.

"No." Her tone slammed him into place, as heavy and inflexible as a whack from a tire iron.

"Excuse me?"

"I'm your bodyguard. I need to come with you. Everywhere."

And didn't that sound enticing. Probably not for her, but for him. Fuck, he'd always enjoyed coming with an attractive woman, being watched by her. Except she hadn't said that sentence to titillate. He doubted she'd read into her words quite like he had — she'd meant the statement as more of a threat. And yet, it still got him going. "Fine. Let's go."

Although small, the supermarket boasted a broad range of products that fit his simple, somewhat gourmet palate. He pushed the trolley up the narrow, crammed aisles with Lexie selecting stuff off the shelves.

Surprisingly, they didn't argue over food. In terms of eating, they had similar tastes — a preference for a range of cheeses, cold meats, fresh fruit and veggies, gluten-free pasta, rice, eggs, beef, pork, lamb, chicken, full-bodied red wine.

They'd just finished paying for their groceries and he glanced up. "Dan! Hey, mate. It's been ages!" Dan Mercurio, a middle-aged guy with that classic 'strawberry' red nose from too much alcohol indulgence, had owned the local supermarket since before Chase had even bought his holiday house several years ago.

The guy's face lit up with a smile and he reached out to shake Chase's hand. "Great to see you. You haven't visited for a while, but I can see why. You've been the golden boy prosecutor, putting away all the riff-raff to keep us citizens safe."

Chase laughed. "Thank you. I do my best to look after the community."

"Who's this lovely lady?"

"Oh, sorry. Ah...Lexie's a friend of mine."

"Is she? Good to meet you." Dan gave him the you-dirty-dog side eye, a gigantic grin on his face.

"You too." Her short, sharp tone and forced smile suggested the exact opposite.

"Are you on holidays?" Dan refocused on him, apparently not noticing Lexie's cold, unenthused response.

"Yeah. I decided to change it up this year. After the last case, I needed a break. It was pretty intense."

"I bet."

The loudspeaker sounded, requesting Dan in aisle five. "Sorry, duty always calls at the most inopportune times."

"Doesn't it?"

The guy hurried off and Lexie elbowed Chase in the side. "Low profile, remember?" she whispered.

He understood that he needed to stay on the down-low as much as possible, but what was he supposed to do? Ignore people he knew? Wouldn't that draw more attention? Make people extra suss, create negative publicity?

They carried the bags to the car, then headed into the kitschy café next door to order a much-needed coffee. Latte for him, short black for her. *Of course.*

For a split second he considered selecting one of his favorite desserts from the tempting array of sweets in the display cabinet—mini lemon meringue tarts, lamingtons, chocolate brownies—but he really didn't need the extra calories, and Lexie couldn't stop fidgeting, obviously eager to leave.

He went to pay and had just tapped his card when Jimmy Broderick, the wiry, outgoing café owner—who'd moved into the area a year ago—came out from the kitchen.

"Chase? What are you doing here, man?"

"Having a well-deserved vacation."

"After that huge case, yeah? Makes sense."

"I thought so."

"Lexie, Jimmy." Chase waved between them.

"Hi," they said at the same time.

She forced that insincere, hurry-the-fuck-up smile again.

"How long will you be in town?" Like Dan, he didn't seem to notice her lack of warmth, lack of interest. Thank fuck, or that could draw more unwanted questions, curiosity, attention.

"I'm not sure yet. I've got some flexibility in my schedule so I'll see how I go."

"Nice. I look forward to seeing you around."

"Same."

A few more locals exited their booths and came to have a chat, and fifteen minutes later he and Lexie left the premises.

As soon as they stepped outside, she threw her empty take-away cup in a close-by bin—while he waited by the car and admired the way her black jeans clung to her swinging hips and sexy rounded ass—and strode straight back up to him. "Did you hear what I said back there?" She kept her voice soft enough so only he could pick it up.

"Yeah."

She rolled her eyes and huffed, as though dealing with a rebellious schoolboy. "How much plainer can I make it? You need to keep well under the radar. You need to make sure you don't attract too much attention. You're supposed to be hiding out here, not plastering a here-I-am, come-get-me target on your back." She shook her head, exasperated. "I'm trying to protect you, protect us, but I can't do that if you let everyone know you're up at your cabin."

He had a sip of his latte, a little cooler than he'd like it, but the double shot of caffeine still hit the required spot. "I'm sorry. It's just...if I don't acknowledge people I know, they'll find it strange and it'll create more gossip."

She blew out a fuck-you're-infuriating breath through her nose. "Okay then, from this point forward, no going out unless absolutely necessary. We'll order groceries and any other supplies online. You'll need to get your head around not personally choosing your meat and fresh produce. We need to stay confined to the cabin, while me and the team work on leads. We need the seclusion to reduce your risk of harm while trying to find the culprit."

Fuck, she looked sexy when she got all forceful and demanding. Pity he couldn't maximize that, utilize the adrenaline-infused opportunity to kiss her, touch her, work off some of the bottled-up energy.

At least he could tap into his imagination. He'd bloody well need it, and a shit-ton of cold showers, if they were restricted to close quarters for an extended period of time.

Chapter Eight

Chase took the most picturesque route up the mountain to his high-country home, neither of them saying another word. She angled herself toward the passenger-side window, crossed her arms and stared outside. At least she'd put her phone away and paid some attention to the stunning landscape.

Surrounded by towering deciduous and myrtle beech trees, eucalypts, and lush green ferns, with glimpses of the majestic mountain range and the odd sighting of wallabies, echidnas and lyrebirds, his rapid heart rate finally settled.

Although he loved this road, he'd chosen to take the harder drive, the extra windy option for her, wanting to expose Lexie to the beauty of Victorian nature. However, how much she daydreamed rather than took in the view, he had no clue.

They finally arrived at his hand-hewn log cabin, and the second he parked, she threw open her door, retrieved her suitcase and stood on the patio. Waiting.

He let them inside, dumped his luggage in the compact, open-plan living area, beside hers, then collected the shopping and lifted the bags onto the bench.

Lexie reappeared from the short corridor. "There's only one bed."

"But it's a king, so there's plenty of room. You can stay on your side and I'll stay on mine, and you won't even know I'm there."

She blew out an I'm-going-to-lose-it breath. "I'll just sleep on the couch."

"I don't recommend it. It's old and uncomfortable, the springs dig into your spine. And I'd hate for you to have back issues and not be able to do your job."

She glared at him as though she believed he'd set the whole thing up. He hadn't. His conscience wouldn't allow him to take advantage of anyone, waste resources and people's time, take away assistance from those legitimately in crisis.

"I'm sorry the accommodation doesn't meet up to your standards, but Alex demanded we head here, not me."

"It's not that, it's just...I expected more room." As in, she'd assumed after seeing his main residence that the cabin would mirror the grand, sumptuous design of his city home. That she'd have her space away from him, her own quarters.

But he'd bought the cabin for simplicity, a retreat away from his regular rat-race, high-flying lifestyle. Somewhere he could fully de-role and totally chill without judgment. Somewhere he didn't have to uphold his media reputation, his lawyer brand. Somewhere he could relax on his own, or with a lady friend. Somewhere he wouldn't be disturbed.

Sometimes he'd given Alex and Sage the keys so they could have a well-earned break together, while he was stuck in the city. He and Alex had come up on their own a few times and hung out, too.

But his mate insisted on bringing his swag and sleeping bag, lighting a bonfire and camping out under the stars...with the close-by benefit of the cabin's kitchen, toilet and shower. So not exactly roughing it, but still providing the opportunity to tap into that back-to-basics guy bonding.

Lexie glanced around the intimate kitchen-dining-living-room area, and out of the windows, taking in the serene, secluded forest. Exactly what had drawn him to the property.

Would she appreciate it? She'd given a totally non-committal answer to his question about whether she enjoyed nature. However, their time together in this isolated location would be the true test.

And, after all, she'd made the decision to restrict them from leaving the premises until she deemed it safe. So she had to accept a portion of the responsibility for them being stuck up here in such close proximity.

"We'll make it work."

She looked at him, her spectacular gray-green eyes clouded with doubt...and resignation. "We have to."

Chase left her staring out of the window and put the shopping away. Then he opened the insulated Esky and placed the leftover scones and meatball sauce onto the bench. "Are you happy with pasta for dinner?"

She swung around, her sexy body backlit by the sun streaming through the window. "Yes. Do you need some help?"

He hadn't expected her to offer. "Just let me know when you're hungry. I brought the leftover sauce from last night so only need to heat it up and cook some fresh pasta. Easy." Plus, he loved pottering around in the kitchen, invoking his inner chef. It redirected and distracted him from any stress.

Was that a shocked-yet-impressed expression on her stunning face?

"Um...I'm okay for now. Can I go and set up in your study?"

"Of course. Do whatever you have to do. Make yourself comfortable, at home. And if you need anything, just ask."

"I will. Thank you." She flashed him the swiftest of smiles, grabbed her bag, and disappeared down the hallway.

While she settled in and organized her workstation, he made a makeshift meal plan for the week, tidied up, and collected some chopped wood from the enclosed back shed for the fireplace. The temperamental weather required him to be prepared.

Early evening, Chase heated the sauce and pan-fried some basil pesto gnocchi. He hadn't seen Lexie since they'd arrived, and as stupid as it sounded, he missed her snarky, sarcastic presence. Maybe because she didn't kowtow to him like most women.

She'd set a silent challenge in his mind, and he'd become almost fixated on making her smile. He turned off the stove and went to let her know dinner was ready, when she almost slammed into him, emerging from the study looking totally wrecked.

"Are you okay?"

"Just tired." She walked past him and slumped onto a bar stool.

Not just tired. Emotionally exhausted, if he had to guess. He wanted to press her further, get clarification, but held back. From what he'd witnessed, if he tried to force an outcome, she'd withdraw, pushing him further away. Strategy was the name of this precarious game.

He returned to the kitchen and hovered behind the bench. "Would you like a drink?"

"Some of that red would be fantastic."

Sounded like she needed an escape as badly as he did. At least he had his cooking—what did she do to relieve the pent-up pressure? A certain inappropriate, self-gratifying image materialized in his mind. Shit, he shouldn't let his thoughts wander down that debaucherous path.

He poured her a generous glass, and one for himself, not missing her gaze following his every move. Out of general observation or subconscious attraction, he had no idea. He wished he knew.

Normally he excelled at reading women. Those that had shown fairly obvious sexually interested signs, anyway. But her...forget it. It was as though she'd erected an impenetrable force field around her beautiful body.

Chase tapped his glass to hers. "To a speedy resolution."

"Cheers." She swallowed a couple of mouthfuls, closed her eyes and moaned. "So good."

The sound of her overt pleasure went straight to his dick. Thank fuck the bench blocked her view of his crotch. Her pride would no doubt prevent her from an overt stare, but sometimes gazes drifted.

And if he gave away the slightest sign of obvious attraction, it'd not only make things awkward but also she'd refuse to share his bed, and he really didn't want either of them to wind up cramped on the couch.

Chase ignored his inner caveman and focused on sense and practicality. He wanted her to feel comfortable and safe first and absolutely foremost.

He had a couple of sips of wine, trying to appear chilled while attempting to tame his over eager cock, then placed his glass down and dished out their dinner.

"This smells great," she said.

"I hope you like it. There's more, if you do."

"Thanks." She sprinkled a heaped spoon of grated Romano cheese onto her meal and shoveled a forkful of pasta into her mouth like a starving woman. And she probably was. They'd eaten breakfast but had only had a coffee for lunch, and that was hours ago.

"Black pepper? Chili flakes?"

She glanced at him, mouth full, and shook her head. "Uh-uh."

Lexie didn't speak much at the best of times let alone around food, by the looks of things. Although he preferred to chat, would like to get to know her better, find out what made this unusual woman tick, it didn't really bother him.

He accepted her for who she was, would happily let her set the pace, and if it came down to it, he could easily carry most of the conversation. From a young age, almost everyone he met had said that he could talk the leg of the sturdiest chair.

And he rather enjoyed seeing a beautiful woman, with absolutely no holds barred, appreciate his cuisine. In fact, he hadn't realized how much of a turn on it was until now.

The last few women he'd gone out with had all chosen some sort of simple salad. It wasn't until after a sequence of dinner dates, he started to see a recurring pattern. A *salad club woman* pattern he wanted to break.

They only ever ate the lowest amount of calories to keep themselves slim. And he got it, got the importance of staying fit and lean, but not at the expense of health. A person needed a comprehensive range of nutrients that lettuce leaves alone couldn't provide.

Chase added some chili flakes and cheese to his bowl and dug into his gnocchi. Oh yeah, not to sound up himself but he'd really nailed the sauce and meatballs this time around.

When they'd finished, she instigated washing up — an unexpected surprise — and then…what next? They still had a few hours to kill before bed. No doubt she'd want to delay how soon they retired for the evening, given the solo-bed situation.

She dried her hands on a fresh tea towel. "Does the TV work?"

"Yeah. It's restricted reception, but I also brought my hard drive. I've got a stack of movies and series downloaded. I'm sure we could agree on something to watch."

"How about you pick a program while I go and have a quick shower?"

"What do you like?"

"True crime, thrillers, some action, arthouse, and period dramas."

Before he could ask any further questions, narrow down the selection, she took off down the corridor to his bedroom — their bedroom for the duration of their stay.

And didn't the thought of her showering, her naked body sluiced by hot water, steaming up the bathroom get him hard.

Fuck. He had to stop fantasizing and focus on their safety. Like she continued to. Back her with what she'd been employed to do. Help out wherever he could to fast-track a successful outcome. Remain professional. Him client, her his assigned 'protector'.

Except, as screwed up as it sounded, part of him didn't want a resolution to his problem too soon. That would mean splitting from Lexie. And although he loved women, could find his next hook up before the end of the night if he wanted to, it'd been a long while since a woman had captured his attention to this degree.

He scrolled through his hard drive.

Hannibal. The series. His favorite to date. Had she seen it? If not, would she like it? Agree to give it a chance? That would determine whether they had another level of compatibility.

No matter what, he'd give her the option to choose some other show because they needed to work together, be in sync as much as possible, and he believed in being open to difference. Plus he had this unexplainable need to please her, which in turn, pleased him.

She re-entered the living area, dressed in a black satin dressing gown that totally covered her from neck to ankle, yet it conformed superbly to her incredibly sexy figure. Her wet hair shone as though she'd washed it, but had straight away secured it into her regular slicked-back, low-bun style. Unfortunately.

She sat on one of the single couches and tucked her feet up under her. "What did you decide?"

"*Hannibal.* Not the movie."

"You have the series?"

"Yeah."

A rare, joyous smile, no trace of the usual sarcasm lit up her serious face. "It's my favorite. Nothing else I've seen has compared."

His exact thoughts. "Are you happy to watch it or would you rather choose something else?"

"Put it on."

Awesome. It had been a while since he'd last seen it and he looked forward to discussing the show in depth with her. "I have popcorn. Do you want some?"

"I'd love some."

Chase started the first season, unconcerned about missing the first few minutes. He could picture each scene, almost knew every word of dialogue by heart.

He grabbed the popcorn maker out of the pantry and filled a large bowl, adding butter and salt. He poured a portion onto a plate for himself, handed the rest to her, and placed a pile of napkins on the coffee table.

She crunched away, totally engrossed in the episode, and he made them coffees from his café-style coffee machine, heated the remaining plain scones and brought them over with cream and jam.

Lexie grabbed the remote and pressed pause. "What are you doing?"

"Making snacks?"

"Thank you, but take it easy. There's only so much I can eat."

"Noted." However, he couldn't help but be a generous host. If there were leftovers, he'd make sure he ate them. But he enjoyed giving his guests variety. And he'd loved her extremely enthusiastic response to his food.

He settled into the single-seater couch nearby, and tried to get absorbed in the show. It had never posed a problem in the past, but with the magnetic, impossible-to-ignore energy bouncing between them, he couldn't concentrate.

Chase suddenly couldn't wait to go to bed. With her. Unfortunately they'd *literally* be sleeping together. But, being in such close proximity, it increased their chances of touching. Much to her dismay, much to his delight.

However, he would never take advantage. An accidental touch was one thing, purposefully breaching boundaries, quite another. He was the sort of guy who only wanted a woman that showed interest in him, one who consented to contact.

Four episodes later, Lexie yawned and stretched. "I think I better get some sleep."

"Me too." Fuck. Had he responded too eagerly? "You…um…go and get sorted and I'll be there in thirty minutes." That should give her enough time, right? She might even be asleep before he slid into bed.

Chase turned off the TV, made sure the windows were closed and the doors locked, cleaned and dried the remaining dishes, then put them away. He glanced at the clock. Seventeen minutes to go. How would he occupy himself? He craved a shower but he needed to get his PJ bottoms from the bedroom.

Actually, no he didn't. He could access the bathroom through a second door off the main hallway, and when he was done, tuck a towel around his waist until he could grab some rarely used sleepwear.

Chase usually slept naked but, given the circumstances, he didn't think she'd appreciate him lying beside her in his birthday suit.

He walked up the passageway and hesitated by the bathroom entrance. No light glowed from beneath the door but he knocked, just in case. He waited for a bit, with no reply, then tentatively twisted the knob and entered the dark, empty space.

Chase switched on the light, the sliding door into the bedroom closed. *Thank fuck.* He didn't want to wake her or make things any more awkward.

He flicked on the mixer tap and undressed while the water warmed up, then stood under the hot spray, allowing the heat to wash off the stress of the day. He would have loved to have gotten himself off, relieve some of the persistent ache in his balls, but he couldn't risk her hearing him, suspecting anything, being only a few meters away.

So instead he thoroughly focused on cleaning every single inch of his skin, adamant he'd make the most of his next alone-time opportunity. Preferably when she showered or had her headphones on while working.

And his dick was still hard-as-fuck. Great. He'd just have to tip-toe into the bedroom, tug on his PJ pants and slip into bed. Without her noticing. Hopefully she had the lamp turned off.

He finished his shower, dried himself and hit the light switch, allowing his eyes some time to adjust to the darkness. Chase checked his phone and activated the torch. Thirty minutes had almost passed.

He eased open the sliding door, and entered his bedroom, a pillow wall beneath the doona, separating their sides, and a bundle of Lexie on the far edge of the bed.

As quietly as possible, he made his way to his bedside drawers and— *Oh no.* He'd stored his pajamas on Lexie's side, because he'd hardly worn them. He couldn't go around there now or else risk waking her up or creeping her out. Shit.

Boxers it is. Definitely better than nothing. Depending on the circumstances. He grabbed a pair and returned to the en suite. He discarded his towel in the dirty-clothes basket and slipped on his snug, cotton undies.

Was she awake? Asleep? A compulsion to check had Chase close to tapping her shoulder, or whispering her name, but if she'd drifted off, he didn't want to disturb her or touch her without permission. He didn't want to breach their working boundaries. They'd already had a long, exhausting day and needed sleep, not a heated debate.

He lay on his side, as gently as a six foot four, ninety kilo guy could, facing away from her, and fucking hoped she didn't wake up to a firsthand feel of his morning wood.

Chapter Nine

Lexie snuggled into the warmth of a big buff masculine body. *Mmm...* She hooked her leg over the guy's waist, and oh! *Good morning!* She'd well and truly gotten lucky last night.

Rousing from a dead-to-the-world sleep, she fluttered her eyes open and...*shit!* Fuck. Not a dream. Not some hot, exceptional one-night stand. Chase! No. No! So much for the pillow wall she'd erected. A lot of fucking good that had done.

She snuck a peek at his face and thank the universe, he remained peacefully asleep. Lexie let out a controlled, incredibly relieved breath and inch by slow, careful inch, attempted to extricate herself from his grasp.

Cautiously nudging and kicking the fallen, scattered pillows to totally clear the path back to her side of the bed, she went to roll away and he shifted, slapping his hand onto her ass and gripping tight. If she attempted to slip from his hold now, she'd wake him for sure. She just had to wait it out.

As soon as he relaxed, she'd take the opportunity to try again to escape from his embrace without him realizing. Lying in his arms under the toasty doona in the interim was nowhere near a huge hardship.

Worst case scenario, if he woke up, she'd feign being asleep, and see how he handled it. Part of her wanted to hold out no matter what, to witness firsthand how he'd react. How he'd respond. Seeing him all embarrassed and lost for words would be so worth it, drop the suave, sophisticated, silver-tongued solicitor down a peg or ten.

She stayed as still as possible and attempted to keep her body lax enough for him to believe she hadn't come close to stirring. And part of that meant she had to stop staring at his face.

But he looked so serene, so boyish, so sweet. Squish-huggable. Add the super enticing scent of his soap — leather and musk, citrus and cedar — and she wasn't going anywhere. Until she had to.

With great reluctance, she tilted her head until she leaned her ear against his smooth, hard chest, his heart beating slow and steady. Soothing, calming, while his ramrod cock, nudging her panty-covered clit, ramped up her arousal.

She swallowed and tried to keep her respiration rate stable, and prevent her pulse from pounding, tried to stop her pelvis from undulating against his. Tried to stop thinking about how hot it would be to rub against him until they each climaxed.

Turned on by Chase? A renowned player? A guy who didn't believe she was skilled enough to protect him, keep him safe? What the fuck was wrong with her? Yes, he was handsome. And insightful and funny. But so the fuck what?

Her fiancé had seemed all those things too and ditched her when it mattered most. Lacked faith in her. Lacked the ability to love. Sure, he'd professed it, but hadn't shown his affection through consistent action. Hadn't shown it when it counted. The guy was the king of lip service.

Physically, she craved a passionate, sweaty fuck. A thorough release. She hadn't had sex for too long, which explained her momentary lapse in her normally clear judgment, the unsolicited lust for her client.

Client! She couldn't forget that. Couldn't forget his concerning, scarily similar traits to her ex-partner. She would not let her body dictate her behavior. Or pay the painful price…a second time.

"Mmm…Lexie." He hauled her against him and clutched her butt tighter.

Oh God. Conflict raged inside her. He felt so deliciously good, and she had no doubt he'd deliver in the bedroom, but she couldn't go there for so many reasons.

Hang on, had he called out her name in his sleep? Was he dreaming about her? A rush of unexpected delight surged straight to her guarded heart. *Don't get carried away.* They were stuck together for who knew how long, so it made sense she might appear in his dreams. But was it only that, or did he actually find her attractive?

It doesn't fucking matter! Though, if it didn't, how come the thought of making a positive impression on him, on Chase possibly desiring her, have her feeling so elated? Ecstatic.

"Couldn't wait to touch me, huh?" His voice rumbled, still laden with the remnants of sleep.

She broke out of his embrace, trying not to get tangled in the quilt, and glared at him, her pulse skyrocketing. "Excuse me? You hugged *me*."

"Then why are you on *my* side of the bed?" He raised his eyebrows, a grin twitching at the corners of his lips.

She went to speak and sputtered, stammered. How could she reply to that without further incriminating herself? "I...I was asleep. Unaware. I must have been cold and rolled over to the hottest spot."

"So you admit you find me hot?"

She wanted to elbow that smirk right down his throat. "You wish."

He chuckled — *smug bastard* — then did a big lion-like stretch, exposing his broad, muscular chest and lickable washboard abs.

"What time is it?" She tried to ignore his mostly naked body and focus on facts. Focus on getting her mind out of its feverish, spellbound, lust-struck state and back to functional. Practical.

He reached over to the bedside table, grabbed his mobile and used fingerprint ID to unlock the screen. Light splashed across his gorgeous, infuriating face. "Almost six-thirty."

"We need to get up."

"I already am."

Oh, she hadn't missed *that*. And he knew she knew. Did he want to suss out her reaction, see if she blushed? See if she admitted she'd felt his impressive morning glory? She faked an annoyed expression and shook her head. "You're such a guy."

Lexie threw back the covers, rummaged through her suitcase, grabbed some fresh underwear and another comfy black outfit with pockets — sneaking in her panty vibrator — and stormed to the en suite. She locked both doors and tried to calm her breathing. *That man.* How could someone rile her up so much while being equally arousing? *Ugh.*

Although he pushed her buttons, he also got her horny. Had her core flaring with an insatiable ache. Not acknowledging it would cause more issues. Knowing how he made her feel would help her more effectively deal with the circumstances, without having to give her stimulated state away. Ultimately, she needed an outlet, a way to release the building tension.

Lexie removed the elastic from her hair and had a much-needed hot shower, luxuriating in the only guaranteed Chase-free minutes she'd have today.

She had to admit, so far, he'd been great at giving her time to herself, her own space to think and problem solve and basically do her job. But once she stepped out of the en suite, the rest of the day, in one way or another, was all about him.

When she'd showered and dressed, placing the panty vibrator in the perfect spot, she brushed her still-wet hair into a low, neat bun, and met him in the kitchen. "What's for breakfast?"

He glanced up, meeting her gaze, his blue eyes penetrating deep. "Anything you don't eat? Any dietary requirements?"

"I'm not a huge fan of garlic. Other than that, I'll have most things."

"Good. Leave it to me."

"Need some help?" She'd love him to help her climax but that was so inappropriate, and well, crazy wrong.

"No. All good."

Phew. If he couldn't assist her, at least he provided her the gift of some time alone to help herself. "Okay, well, I'll…um, go and get some work done."

"No worries. I'll call out when the food's ready."

She restrained her smile and controlled her steps to a stroll when all she wanted to do was fist-pump the air and run to the study to get started on satisfying her desperate desire for an orgasm.

Lexie entered the compact workspace, kept the door ajar to ensure she'd be able to hear his voice, sat on the office chair and leaned against the back. She logged onto her laptop, fished the panty vibrator remote out of her pocket and watched the door while she cycled through vibration settings. She had to hurry — she had to come quickly.

Lexie found her favorite buzzy option, adjusted her position to maximize the vibe, and closed her eyes.

Bliss.

Unbidden images of Chase flooded her brain and the harder she tried to tune them out, the harder they came.

Him doing her against the wall, him taking her from behind on the bed, his dick buried to the hilt, her hair wrapped around his hand and him tugging, adding a slightly painful edge to the pleasure.

That did it. She climaxed, the intensity greater than what she'd experienced in a long time. The remote fell to the floor and she cried out, bucking into the seat. She gasped and slapped her hand against her mouth.

She snapped her eyes open and darted her gaze to the door to find Chase standing in the entrance, leaning against the architrave, a smirk on his exasperatingly hot face.

Too late. Shit. How much had he heard? How much had he seen?

"Enjoy yourself?"

She tried to look unaffected, neutral. "How long have you been standing there?"

"Long enough."

Fuck. "What are you doing here?" She raised her eyebrows in accusation.

"I came to check if you like mushrooms…but it looks like you already came."

Her face flared with heat. With her fair skin, no way could he miss her telltale fuchsia blush.

Chase prowled toward her, slowly, carefully, his stare unwavering, and crouched beside her left leg. Within easy touching distance. What the hell…? Her heart thudded against the confines of her ribcage, begging to break free. So loud. Could he hear?

He handed her the panty-vibrator remote. "I think you dropped this." Then he sprang up and left her to recover.

She slumped against the backrest and blew out a relieved breath. He could have gone harder, ribbed her to the max, possibly even accused her of being unprofessional, but he didn't.

He'd had a bit of fun, but ultimately demonstrated by his actions that, at some level, he respected her feelings, the complexity of their forced-proximity living arrangement, and the importance of having a bodyguard.

The guy's high-end observational skills made her nervous, like he could virtually read her thoughts, but also proved useful when it came to understanding the nuances and intricacy of situations. It showed signs of empathy. A trait she hadn't believed he possessed.

* * * *

Thankfully over the next week, he never mentioned the panty vibrator faux pas again, and they had no more surprise intimate encounters. The larger pillow barrier she'd erected between them in bed, plus ensuring she stayed on the farthest side of the mattress, sleeping with virtually one eye open, helped, as did her more strategic vibrator usage—timing it for when he went for a shower or to chop wood.

Chase continued to make their morning meals— something different every day, ranging from pancakes, to bacon and eggs, to muffins, to a full English breakfast, to a Continental breakfast, to homemade granola, to smashed avocado and eggs on toast.

All tempting, all delicious. All irresistible. And if she didn't watch it, she'd stack on the weight. This was the most sedentary job she'd had, while increasing her regular calorie intake and mental stimulation. Having the added burst of nutrition had apparently helped with her attention and concentration. Pros and cons. In the end it all came down to balance.

They fell into a somewhat workable routine. After they ate, Lexie sat in the study, and to his credit, Chase didn't dare bother her to discuss anything, without clear advance warning. While she worked, he cleaned the cabin, cooked, cut and collected wood in the enclosed backyard, and followed up any pressing attorney stuff.

Even with the undeniable electricity zinging between them, he didn't attempt to make a move, which she appreciated yet found equally disappointing. Ridiculous. How could she find someone like her ex attractive? She had to be a masochist.

No matter how much she tried to rationalize her way out of her feelings, from a lust perspective, she couldn't deny she wanted him. And she could sense he wanted her too, but both of them held back.

From her side, getting together didn't make sense because they had to work as a partnership, they couldn't allow their emotions to compromise their safety, and last but not at all least, she couldn't get involved with another self-righteous, self-serving player.

She couldn't seriously sustain any sort of interest in someone who questioned her skills, didn't understand what her job meant to her, how much significance it held in her life.

Oh, he kept up his smart-ass comments and innuendo, but nothing that rang dodgy alarm bells. Outside of that she had several hours of alone time, within the close confines of his cozy cabin. And much to her surprise, it was comfortable.

She hadn't felt this relaxed in, well, ages. Aside from the peaceful surroundings allowing her to recharge, away from the daily barrage of people, her panty vibrator also played a huge part in helping her cope.

Though *relaxed* wasn't quite the right word. More like a lit sparkler that grew brighter and brighter and more intense the more it burned. Which probably meant this unacknowledged attraction between them would fizzle out just as quickly. As expected with a guy like him.

Aside from this, it could possibly compromise her ability to do her job with the utmost integrity. Reinforcing exactly why she'd kept her distance. Why she continued to act cool, disinterested, unaffected.

Overall he'd behaved just as considerately, not physically overstepping, except she'd glimpsed the banked desire in his eyes any time they were within arm's reach. Which was often. Much more frequently than she'd anticipated or prepared for, emotionally, psychologically. Had he seen I-want-you signs in her too?

Thankfully, since they'd relocated to this reasonably remote area, there'd been no other threats. Though, part of her wished they'd had a few to narrow down suspects, solve the case and get her away from the growing sexual temptation.

This morning, however, Chase seemed extra twitchy. Unable to sit or even stand still, he paced about the kitchen like a shaken-up can of soda ready to burst, his breath shunting in and out of his lungs.

"What's wrong?" She kept her eyes on him and scooped up another spoonful of his homemade granola mixed with Greek yoghurt.

If he kept charging up and down the same set of floorboards, he'd wear a channel into the timber. "I need to get out of here."

"Go and chop some more wood. Out the back." The enclosed area with high fences provided the safest spot, second to staying indoors.

"I need more than that." He stopped and fidgeted, shoving his hands through his thick, usually perfect hair.

Far from perfect today. Today the strands looked ruffled, standing up on end at all sorts of odd angles.

"I need some space, some freedom. I feel like a caged animal." He stared at her, his hair mussed, his brow creased, his face filled with anguish.

She conjured up her clearest, calmest voice. "Until the assailant is found, unfortunately you're restricted. We both are. You know that."

He planted his palms on the benchtop and leaned forward, his penetrating gaze never leaving her eyes. "I know that I have a raging case of cabin fever and I need some fresh air."

"Or what?"

"I'll lose my shit." His voice hung heavy with desperation. He pushed back up into standing and thrust his hands through his hair again. Once, twice, three times. "I usually engage in conversation all day, and I'm not getting that need met."

"You're such an extrovert." She tried to inject some humor into the situation but the distressed look in his eyes showed he'd gone way past appreciating her lighthearted attempt at de-escalation.

"Yeah, I am. And I need stimulation. Regular interactions with people."

The opposite of her. Computer contact didn't do it for him, whereas it easily met her peopling requirements. She liked some social time too, but in small, controlled doses, broken up by recuperation, re-energizing solitary time. "You talk to me."

"But that's only when you can fit me in." He started pacing again, stopped and scrubbed his hands over his face. "I swear, I'm not ungrateful. I know you're busy, focused on helping me, so I try my best not to distract you.

"I understand you need to do your job, and I'm doing everything I can to provide the space and sustenance you need as well as retain my role remotely, but it's not the same as what I'm used to. And I'm struggling."

Oh. His unexpected honesty hit her right in the heart, like a solid steel sledgehammer. Her inner urge pushed her to give him a hug, but she couldn't. Shouldn't. Wouldn't.

It would only complicate things, blur their already fuzzy boundaries. Her introverted perspective hadn't considered how their confinement would impact someone like him.

Chase had upheld his part of their bargain, had been super supportive to her in the midst of all the turmoil and uncertainty. So she needed to push out of her comfort zone and ask how she could assist him...within reason. "Is there something I can do to help?"

"Actually, yeah."

Her pulse took off like an Olympic sprinter. Should she have asked such an open question? What would he suggest?

Didn't matter. She could always say *no* if she didn't agree, and offer another alternative. Right?

"I need a run."

"I'm sorry?"

"A run, a hike. Something physical. I need to expend some energy. There's a track that does a circuit around my property. Power walking, it should take less than forty-five minutes, running, twenty-five. It's totally camouflaged by trees so I won't be in any danger."

"You don't know that."

"Unless it's someone from town who knows me and where I live or someone's followed us, I'm sure I'll be fine."

They still had no idea who could be behind this whole thing or what the person knew, hence why they'd taken the strictest precautions. But given his mini meltdown, she needed to find a compromise. "I'm not letting you go on your own."

"Why not? It'll allow you some undisturbed work time while I sweat off some of my stress."

"I told you. The assailant could be anyone. Could be someone you know. We can't take that chance. So you need to be cautious. As Alex instructed, anytime you leave here, I need to be right beside you. Ideally, I need to accompany you everywhere. It's my job. I need to protect you. Make sure you don't do anything stupid."

Would her response offend him? Make him feel as though she questioned his ability to make a sound decision? That she had treated him like a naughty, untrustworthy child she had to keep in check?

He stared her straight in the eye. "Well then, come with me."

Uh-uh. She didn't run. She did the exercise bike and the occasional skipping and weights but running, jogging? No. Just no. "Can't you use your treadmill, exercise bike or elliptical machine in the shed?"

"Not the same. They're still inside and I need oxygen, the outdoors, nature. That's why I bought this place. If I wanted to remain cooped up indoors, I'd have stayed in town and used my personal gym. Believe me, exercising outside is totally different." He wrung his hands, his face tight, creases slashing his forehead.

A wave of uneasiness crashed in her stomach, yet she couldn't deny him. They didn't know how much longer they'd be stuck in the cabin, and if she didn't provide him the opportunity to let off some building catastrophic steam, he'd explode. Or make a careless decision. "Fine. Give me five."

Chapter Ten

Lexie brushed her teeth, changed into a short-sleeved black top, leggings and runners, and concealed her gun in a back holster.

She re-entered the living area and his eyes practically bugged out of his head like a cartoon character. "What?" She glanced down at herself. Did she have a stain on her outfit? Had she inadvertently exposed a nipple? Or her pistol?

Or had he purely appreciated her active wear? The way her breasts filled out the V-neck T-shirt, creating a noticeable cleavage, and how the tight stretchy pants clung to the shape of her legs? Highlighted her assets.

He wrenched his gaze away and grabbed his keys off a set of hooks by the door. "Nothing. Let's go."

O-kay.

They stepped out into the chilly morning air, and she inhaled the soothing scent of eucalyptus. A chorus of birds trilled and combined with the native animal sounds, they acted as a relaxation tonic.

Blue sky stretched in a one-hundred-and-eighty-degree arc over the cabin, and the sun beamed through branches of the surrounding dense bushland. The lush green plants and towering trees, particularly the eucalypts, looked and smelled amazing, inviting, invigorating. She could suddenly see why he'd chosen this spot.

He locked up, closed his eyes and took a slow, deep breath, then met her gaze. "Ready?" He smiled for the first time that morning.

"For a hike, yes. Running, not so much."

He laughed. So refreshing to hear after his mini freak out. "Okay. Hike it is. Follow me."

The guy had fucking long legs, his stride one to two of her steps. She had to virtually jog to keep up. So much for not having to run.

A few minutes in and a whoosh whizzed by Chase's head, bark cracking and splintering as a bullet burrowed into a nearby tree. *Fuck!* She yanked him to the ground but instead of staying safely beneath her, he rolled on top, keeping himself way too exposed. Stupid fucking ego-driven macho shit.

She thrashed against his hard muscular torso, trying to resume her protective position but he wouldn't let her. So fucking frustrating, infuriating. Did the guy realize how much he was at risk? Had he not worked that out already? Chase was the target, not her.

If her arms weren't pinned underneath him, she'd have decked the guy...for his own safety. Did he understand how much his bull-headed resistance impacted his life and potentially her career?

She wriggled some more, attempting with every ounce of energy to throw him off, but no chance. The man was a fucking lean-ass beast. And although he'd made a fucking-idiot move, his big body pressing down on hers felt undeniably divine.

But they needed to go. Now. If they remained out here a moment longer, they'd be catatonic sitting ducks. Impossible to miss. "Get off me." She growled, her teeth clenched together, her tone deceivingly soft, yet menacing.

His brow puckered, but he shifted. As though her words had jolted him out of his hero haze and back to the urgency of the moment.

It did the trick, him rolling to the side and staying low. Thank fuck. "Head back inside…"

He went to leave and she grabbed his T-shirt. "But keep crouched, close to the ground. Understand?"

Chase nodded. "Yeah. Are you coming?"

She almost had, from the pure friction of their bodies. "Just go. I'll meet you back there," she whispered, hoping whoever had taken the shot hadn't hung around, couldn't hear their conversation, wouldn't make another attempt.

Thank the fucking universe, he followed her command, and she moved onto her knees, gun drawn, ready to fire. Ducking down, he crept along the path back to the cabin. Exposed for what felt like an eternity.

Fuck, she should have warned him to check for any intruders. She jumped up with well-trained, stealthy ease, brushed herself off, and followed him with brisk yet cautious steps.

She darted her eyes in a full arc around the surrounding tall trees, shiny green ferns, and open expanse leading to his holiday house, hurrying to rejoin him and ensure his wellbeing. Ensure she did her job. Ensure they both stayed alive.

No unusual glints of sunshine highlighted anyone close-by with a gun, suggesting the perpetrator had taken off. Or had it holstered. Hopefully they weren't waiting for them inside the cozy, innocent-looking cottage.

She snuck through the door, and snicked it shut. Chase went to speak, and she held her finger to her lips in a *shhh* motion. Thank fuck he didn't argue, and followed her instructions. She mouthed *stay here* and he nodded.

Keeping her gun raised and outstretched, Lexie thoroughly checked every single room. No one. Nothing out of place. His high-country home appeared safe...for the moment.

She breathed out a long sigh of relief, packed her revolver away, and rejoined Chase in the living area. Going forward, she'd need to include an external sweep of the perimeter of the property first thing each morning, and on her breaks.

Chase stood, staring out of the front window.

Still wired, and wanting to make certain he understood the seriousness of his stupidity, she slammed her hand on the bench causing him to startle. "What the fuck were you thinking?"

He spun around to face her. "I..." He clenched his jaw, a muscle ticking in the corner of his angular face, his expression a mix of unexpressed words bound with guilt and remorse.

"How you responded screams you still don't trust me? But Alex fucking does. Your best mate, an expert in the field, hired me, believes in me, why can't you?" She shouldn't shout. It didn't help, but she couldn't stop herself.

"I..." He stared back at her, totally inarticulate. Fumbling for an answer. A first for him, she imagined. The guy was normally full of words, explanations, arguments.

"If you have a problem with me, speak to Alex. Otherwise, I'll be here, doing what I do best, doing my job. But please, *please*, don't make it harder because you have some fucking white-knight complex."

Chase stalked toward her, his long strides eating up the space in seconds. With a determined, unwavering look in his eye, he grabbed her face with both hands and slammed his lips onto hers.

Fuck. So unexpected, so hot. She should stop him, stop herself, but fuck he could kiss.

She didn't want to play games, though. Didn't want to fall victim to an adrenaline rush, the need for a quick fuck, a quick endorphin fix. Couldn't afford to succumb to the compulsion for releasing her primal pressure valve.

She'd been there, done that several times with her ex-fiancé, who in the end had happily, easily broken things off when it had mattered. When she'd needed the most support. To prevent a repeat of the past, she couldn't allow anything to screw up her ability to enforce their current and future safety.

Lexie gathered up enough strength to push him away, and studied his eyes, the gorgeous blue eclipsed by black. Fear? Desire? A combination of the two?

"Don't fuck with me." Why had she said that with so much venom? Bloody emotions. Bloody unresolved associations to her narcissistic, selfish, manipulative ex.

"I'm not." He stood back and shoved his hand through his hair. "Sorry, I...I can't stand the thought of you getting hurt because of me."

Lexie thrust her hands on her hips. "Well, get over it. I was hired to protect you, remember? It goes with the territory."

A deep frown split his brow.

She glared at him, still not quite finished with her tirade. "And kissing me to alleviate some of your stress, to ensure you get your physical outlet, doesn't hurt anyone?"

"It's not like that."

She raised an explain-yourself eyebrow. "Then how is it?"

"I'm relieved you're okay. That we're both okay." He went to lean in.

"So, you'd kiss anyone out of relief?"

"What?" His forehead crinkled up like a sheet of corrugated iron and he stopped, his eyes searching hers. "No! No." He shook his head. "I care about you. I don't want you harmed."

"I don't want either of us harmed, and I'll do everything to prevent it, but, as I said, with my line of work comes risk."

"Doesn't mean I have to like it. Doesn't mean I can step back and put you in danger."

"You have to find a way to learn to accept it." She huffed out a breath. How could she get through to him that if he took matters into his own hands he'd potentially increase the likelihood of injury to both of them. "The more you ignore it, the more you put yourself in unnecessary danger. And by doing that, I could end up as collateral damage.

"This person doesn't give a toss about *me* specifically. Do you hear what I'm saying? How much clearer can I be? They want to see *you* suffer. And they'll do whatever it takes to get to *you*. The more you try and be a hero, the more likely we'll both be killed."

"But I can't stop myself from caring." He touched her face so gently, so tenderly, unwelcome tears swelled behind her eyes.

She averted her gaze and blinked back the acidic moisture threatening to undo her resolve. "Why? How can you put your life on the line for your paid security guard, for *me*, when we've only known each other just over a week?"

"Time is irrelevant. It's about connection. And we have it."

"Do we?" Her voice came out all what-the-fuck husky. Where did he intend to go with this?

He tipped her chin up and studied her eyes. "Don't tell me you can't feel it. If you say you don't, you're lying."

Fuck. Fuck him. Although painful to admit—he was right. No way could she deny it. His highly attuned observational skills would alert him, ring don't-bullshit-me alarm bells if she even tried.

The magnetism had pinged between them almost from the moment they met. Strangely, bizarrely. They had so many differences and yet...

None of their mutual attraction made logical sense. But when was lust ever rational? "Okay, I confess—I do. But there's one thing feeling something and another, acting on it. We're adults with executive thought, we understand the importance of discipline, and we're working together."

"So?" His eyes briefly dipped to her mouth. "That's separate. You have no control of when or how you meet the right person. When things click, they click."

The right person? What the fuck? She locked her gaze on his. "My first priority is to keep you safe, not fool around."

"Is that what you think this is?"

She swallowed and tried to stay firm, but with him so near she struggled not to close the small distance between them and resume their core-melting kiss. "Yeah. I know your type."

"And what's that?" His body hovered over hers, his lips so damn tempting.

"A womanizer, a player. Someone who strives for short-term fun, who always makes sure they get their needs met."

"You really believe I'm that guy?" His face contorted with surprising sadness and disappointment.

"I haven't seen anything to refute it. You don't even trust me to protect you. You see me as some woman, out of her depth, who needs you to look after her. Some damsel in distress to stroke your fragile ego."

"You've got it so wrong. I intervened because I *fucking* care. I know we've only known each other a short time but some things are clear." He huffed out a breath. "Don't assume I don't give a fuck. Don't assume I'm taking advantage, that I want to use you for some 'physical outlet'." He pressed his palm to his chest like a pledge. "I swear I'm being straight up, that I don't have some covert, self-serving agenda."

Lexie stayed silent, trying to assess if his words matched his body language. She must have looked unconvinced because he sighed and shook his head.

"Do you really think I'd put myself at risk to prove a point? I did it because you mean something to me."

"You sure it wasn't to alleviate some of that escalating stress? Desperation and stupidity can mimic honorable intention."

He scrubbed his hand over the scruff on his face, all rough and frustrated, his teeth clenched, his jaw flexing, and stared at her with complete conviction. "Have you not heard anything I've said? What I did had nothing at all to do with desperation or stupidity."

Oh. *Oh.* Who'd have thought a guy like him could *actually* consider someone else? Experience such heartfelt emotions? Or did he? The man could talk and had mastered the corresponding behavioral nuances, perfecting his physical gestures and responses so they aligned with his words.

His profession had helped him hone his charm and develop elite speaking and body language skills over the years, as evidenced by his high prosecutor case win rate.

He'd shown a history of saying the right thing for the given moment and backing it with action. Had he used those strategies with her, or did he truly mean what he'd admitted?

Had honesty driven his decision to divert down this discussion path or had his choice been a strategic move, providing another way for him to achieve the real outcome he wanted?

With his outside exercise plan cut short, he hadn't received the required relief, but maybe he'd accomplish the same result, possibly an even better one, from a quick, sweaty screw.

He obliterated what remained of her personal space and firmly held her face, making sure she looked into his eyes. "I'm not fucking you around." Had he tapped into her thoughts? Or maybe the telltale, hidden signs in her mannerisms? Maybe both. Either way, his ability to read people was fucking scary…and alluring.

Chase could spout off anything he wanted, but for her to fully believe him, trust him, his behavior had to consistently correlate with each and every sentence.

His eyes and posture and facial expression said, *I'm not bullshitting you*, but she didn't know him well enough to recognize any signature quirks that might give away whether he told the entire truth.

"Say something." His tone virtually pleaded. "Please." He searched her eyes as though they'd reveal an additional clue to her current mindset.

He looked so believably honest, so hopeful, so vulnerable. Her biggest weak spot. Lexie threw her arms around his neck and slammed against him, unable to resist the guy — or his sensual mouth — any longer.

Chase responded instantly, eagerly, thrusting his tongue between her lips, licking and teasing and sucking. And driving her horniness up to red-line level.

The desperation coming from both sides had her climbing him like a tall, tantalizing tree. He yanked the elastic tie from the base of her head, setting her hair free.

"Beautiful." Chase raked his fingers through her long black locks, and gripped her ass with his other hand, holding her firmly to him. He resumed the kiss and it soon heated up to nuclear explosive.

Just like he had in her fantasy, he pressed her against the closest living room wall, and rubbed his deliciously hard dick against her clit. She gasped and moaned as he traveled his lips down the column of her neck, licking and kissing and nipping.

And it felt beyond amazing, lighting up every single nerve ending. But they needed less clothes. She needed him inside her. Now. She ran her hand along his hot body, slipped it beneath his sweatpants and boxers and stroked.

He groaned and thrust into her palm, pre-cum providing her just the right amount of lubrication to easily slide over his huge erection. Up and down, up and down, up and down.

She bit right where his neck met the corded muscle in his torso and he growled and stilled her hand. "Take off your pants, and I'll grab a condom."

"No."

He stared into her eyes, his brow creased with confusion. "No? You want to stop?"

"No." *Definitely fucking not.* "I want you. I can't wait. I'm on the pill and I'm STI free. You?"

"I'm all clear too."

She lowered her legs from his waist and stood, kicking off her runners and shedding her leggings and panties in seconds.

His eyes darted to her pussy and he looked utterly mesmerized.

No time for admiration. They could do that later. Her aching core dictated she needed to get off. And she imagined his cock concurred. So she resumed her position, her legs wrapped around his hips, an arm around his neck, and grabbed his dick, guiding him to her slick entrance.

Instantly, he thrust into her and, *fuck me*, filled her right up. She clung tighter to him and leaned her head against the wall. Fuck, he felt good. Nothing beat real cock for a full sensory experience.

Chase locked his lips on hers and kissed her beyond senseless, while delving his dick deep, pushing her way too quickly to the brink. But the benefit of being a thoroughly turned-on woman meant she could let go and come again in moments.

Going by the way his erection slid along every one of her pleasure points, she'd come like a fucking freight train in seconds. And climax again. And again. And again.

She'd orgasmed a couple of times in a row with men in the past, and had gotten off on multiple occasions with her toys. Could he make her come close to her history of ultimate orgasms? Exceed what she'd experienced?

Chase increased his fucking pace, nailing her hard, his lips never once leaving hers. He'd totally taken over her body, held her captive, in the absolute best possible way.

She arched into him and cried out, coming all over his cock, her fingertips digging into his T-shirt covered traps. He grunted, and followed her into orgasmic bliss. And she came again, crying out in shameless, unrestrained ecstasy.

He fucked her right through to the end of their combined pleasure and buried his head into her shoulder, his hot breath penetrating her top and pelting against her perspiring skin.

Although she'd fought against succumbing, she couldn't deny that nothing exceeded the urgency, the desperation, the excitement of an adrenaline-fueled fuck.

Their breathing started to slow and he lifted his head and looked her in the eye. "Wait right here, okay?"

Lexie nodded, unable to move even if she wanted to, and he pulled out. She lowered her still-trembling legs to the timber. He waited, keeping hold of her as though to make sure she didn't topple over following her epic series of climaxes.

Although a little wobbly, she could take her weight. Just. "I'm fine."

He searched her eyes. "You sure?"

"Yes." Well, pretty sure.

"Stay put." He tucked his dick back in his pants and padded down the hallway.

Chapter Eleven

Did he seriously worry she might take off? Where would she go? The next room? She couldn't get too far unless she totally abandoned him, abandoned her new career. And she couldn't do either of those things.

Plus, going by their chemistry, some regular fucking might help them positively pass the time...as long as neither of them got too attached. His history suggested he wouldn't have that problem. But she needed to check herself. Constantly. She didn't want to set up anything that had unrealistic emotional expectations.

She hoped she could uphold a detached view, separate sex from love, but... Bloody hormones had a way of screwing her over, developing an attachment, a yearning for commitment.

Her problem. Not his. And if she couldn't deal with it, she should stop things right now. Make sure it didn't happen again.

Chase returned with a wet washcloth and kneeled in front of her. "Spread your legs."

She sucked in a breath and did as he asked. He proceeded to pat her pussy with the warm, damp flannel, thoroughly, reverently, cleaning away their combined cum. And fuck it felt so nice, soothing yet arousing.

He threw the now-cool dirty cloth aside and glanced up. "Take off your top. I need to see you. Fully."

And she wanted him to. Wanted to assess his response. Slowly, with as much sex appeal as she could muster, she lifted her T-shirt over her head and dumped it on the floor, then unhooked her bra and dropped it on top.

"Fuck me." His hungry eyes devoured her body, getting her all hot and horny, ready to go again.

"I believe I just did."

A wicked-as-fuck smile tugged at the corners of his sinful mouth. "You did indeed. And it was fucking fantastic. But I'm getting withdrawal. It's time for round two."

Chase held her hips and kissed her bellybutton piercing, then trailed his lips to her clit ring and gave it a flick with his tongue, sending waves of pleasure straight to her core.

"So sexy." His deep voice had turned extra raspy, extra rumbly, extra alluring.

Fingers crossed he didn't intend to just tease her with kisses and light strokes. Lexie had fully recovered from her string of climaxes and needed more. She'd quickly passed the point of patience.

She needed his mouth buried between her thighs, determined to find out if his tongue was as talented in the licking and sucking department as it was with talking.

Weaving her fingers through his thick blond hair, she thrust into his face, silently begging for him to go harder, faster, deeper.

He tapped her outer thigh. "Lift your leg over my shoulder."

Fuck yes!

She hooked her ankle around his neck, fully exposing her pussy, and angled her pelvis to line up her clit with his mouth.

He inhaled, closed his eyes and sighed. "Fuck, you smell good."

Lexie pressed against his lips, begging for him to stop speaking and delve right in. She couldn't wait to see how well his first attempt matched up to her best-ever oral. So far no guy had outshone the licking and sucking expertise of a woman she'd hooked up with during an experimental phase in her early twenties.

With a flat, soft tongue, he licked slowly from her entrance all the way to the front of her pussy and she almost shot to the ceiling.

"Mmm...so swollen, so wet, so responsive."

So fucking worked up, he only had to swipe his thumb across her clit and she'd climax. He must have sensed it—not surprising, given his extensive array of female conquests—and eased off, working the rest of her super-sensitive folds with his tongue and fingers, keeping her right on the edge.

"Ple-ase."

"Please what?"

She fisted handfuls of his hair. "I need to come. I'm so close."

"What will get you there?"

Lexie shamelessly held his head plastered to her pelvis. "Your mouth on my clit."

"Is that all? How about this?" He collected some of her juices on two fingers and slid them into her ass.

"Yes!" *Oh yes!* The taboo move had the man bursting right out of the constrictive vanilla box she'd confined him to. Anal play, especially while receiving oral, always got her going. It had a way of enhancing every little sensation.

"And this?" He thrust his thumb in her entrance. So delightfully full. Not as good as his cock, but a close second. Add the clit and anal stim and it bumped the experience up to top spot.

She closed her eyes and moaned, past the point of forming meaningful words. Past the point of doing anything except absorbing herself in his incomparable pleasure.

"Eyes on me. I want you to watch me get you off." Given his indisputable gift of the gab, it shouldn't surprise her that he'd excel at dirty talk too. But it did.

She snapped her eyes open, and what a sight. He sat back on his heels, his face partially hidden between her legs, his spectacular blue eyes penetrating hers, and his fingers and thumb pumping inside her at a regular rhythm.

He tongued her clit once, twice, then took the engorged little nub in his mouth and sucked. She came instantly. Her leg shook and he braced her hip with his free hand, keeping her steady, upright, allowing her to enjoy the entire duration of her bone-melting orgasm. No wonder women flocked to him. Sexually, he knew how to please. Knew his way around the female form with undeniable proficiency.

Slowly, carefully, he removed his fingers and thumb from within her body and pressed a kiss above her clit piercing. "Fuck, you taste great."

"Thank you." Always good to hear. She made an effort to eat well, keep fit, and effectively groomed. And going by her lovers' consistent responses, it paid off.

"Thank *you*." He got up, still fully dressed, his dick bulging in his pants, while she stood there naked. Interestingly she didn't feel self-conscious, in fact, it didn't bother her at all.

Chase had shown nothing but appreciation of her, of her power-packed, curvaceous body, her petite hourglass figure far from a super-slim waif. But her research showed he liked a wide range of women.

Pressing his chest against hers, he took her lips in a scorching-hot kiss. He pulled back, swept her hair off her shoulder and brushed his lips across the juncture of her neck and continued up to her ear.

Were full-body orgasms possible? Because almost anywhere he touched shot her straight back into climax territory. Her legs shook in an attempt to keep her standing, and he stopped, as though he noticed her struggling. His beautiful blue eyes sparkled — well, the circle surrounding his dilated pupils — and he intertwined their fingers together. "Let's take this to the bedroom."

She shouldn't. She *really* shouldn't. But her body already craved him again. And by the looks and sounds of things, he wanted her again too. So she let him lead her to the bed they'd shared for the past week.

She swept the pillow barrier aside and lay in the middle of the mattress, facing him. "Everything off."

The dirtiest smile slid onto his lips and he complied, toeing off his sneakers, whipping his T-shirt over his head, and shucking his pants and boxers in one swift sequence. She couldn't stop her eyes from wandering over every single inch of his super fit body.

Even before he'd gotten naked, Lexie could tell he looked after himself by the way his clothes conformed to his physique. However, she hadn't expected he'd have such an athletic, lean, muscular build, his abs and chest and arms so defined. And the biggest surprise of all—she hadn't anticipated he'd pack such a beast of a cock. Thick and long and large.

"Do I meet your standards?"

No. He exceeded them. Physically, and in the lover department, anyway. "You'll do."

He laughed.

"Join me?"

"You can count on that." He climbed onto the bed and hovered beside her. "Lie on your back." She did, and he positioned himself between her legs. "Have you ever come from breast play?"

"No."

"Want to give it a go?"

Oh. She'd assumed he'd want to fuck again rather than spend more time focused on her satisfaction. No previous partner had ever suggested it, never apparently had the patience or generosity, but with the opportunity presenting itself, why not? She had absolutely nothing to lose. And every pleasurable moment to gain. Worst case scenario, he'd work her right up, touch her clit and she'd come. "Sure."

Chase commandeered her mouth in an X-rated kiss and licked to her ear, where he nipped and sucked her earlobe, and continued down her throat to her breast. "You have the sexiest nipples. Fucking gorgeous."

He tweaked one between his finger and thumb, while he sucked on the other. Then alternated. Back and forth, back and forth, back and forth, driving her insane with the need for release, but keeping her on the brink.

"Touch my clit." She blurted the words without warning. A purely lustful, I-need-to-get-off-now response.

"No."

"No?" What? She needed to orgasm so badly. Couldn't he tell? He'd seemed incredibly in tune with her body beforehand.

Chase stopped taunting and teasing, and looked her directly in the eye. "Don't get me wrong. I want to. You're so sexy when you come. I can't imagine anything better than rubbing you, licking you, burying my face down there for hours, but we agreed to breast play only. And the thought of that alone making you climax gets me so hot."

Oh. *Oh God.* She arched up into him. From their sexual interplay to this point, he'd shown a love and appreciation of her body, had virtually worshipped her, as though prioritizing her enjoyment over and above his own. Such a turn on.

So why hadn't women stayed with Chase? Why had he chosen not to commit? He had charisma, intelligence, could cook, clean, was self-sufficient, had a great career, had incredible skills as a lover.

Maybe because of his apparent variety-is-the-spice-of-life mentality? Maybe because he got bored quickly? Maybe, like her, he had a strong drive to protect his heart so stuck to fun, safe, superficial encounters.

Maybe he wanted to protect himself against opportunistic women keen on accessing his money and giving their career a boost? Maybe he used all his energy interacting with people as part of his job and needed uninterrupted down time? Maybe he hadn't met a woman who understood and accepted the huge part work played in his life.

A lot of possible maybes, but all potentially relevant.

He caressed her breast and rolled her nipple between his forefinger and thumb. "So what do you want to do?"

"Keep going? I'm curious too."

His delighted grin sent tingles of... No. She didn't even want to acknowledge it. Couldn't afford to. She had to focus on the physical.

Using his tongue and lips and thumb and fingers, Chase resumed his attentive breast play, making sure to vary up the type and intensity of stimulation on each side, while preventing the rest of her erogenous zones from seeking a quick, short-term fix.

He persevered, and persevered, and if she wasn't so worked up and desperate to come, she'd have appreciated his patience. "Please, Chase, please."

He must have heard the agony in her tone because he upped, well, everything—pace, pressure, speed— and torture turned to bliss.

A different sort of orgasm, more like a mind-gasm, spiraled through her body, setting her core alight with ecstasy. And although relief floated through her like the calm following a severe storm, she still craved his cock.

"Fucking hot." He studied her, a pleased-with-himself grin on his face, then dove in for a kiss.

She agreed. One of the most unexpected, hottest things she'd done, and she'd done a lot. Normally, she'd give in to her desire for release but he'd helped her push past her impatience. The earth-shattering result was so worth the extended wait.

Lexie locked her lips onto his and used the leverage techniques she'd practiced in her police and defense training courses to flip him onto his back. She straddled his hips, his dick throbbing with need. "Blow job, or do you want to fuck?"

He contemplated the options for a couple of seconds, or maybe that was how long it took his brain to reboot. "Fuck."

She grabbed his cock and rubbed it between her legs, coating the monster of a thing with her juices before sliding onto it. Tingles shot to her sex and she threw her head back and moaned. Although the previous position had had her body tingling right down to her toes, this exceeded it, sparking full-blown euphoria in each and every cell.

Lexie could control the tempo, intensity and angle of penetration so his dick stroked right where she needed it, stimulating all her special spots. She undulated her hips and squeezed her core in a slow sensual rhythm that had them both panting and groaning.

After a few minutes, he gripped her hips and thrust up into her fast and full-on furious. She pressed her palms onto his chest, the angle tugging on her clit ring with each grind of her pelvis, and met his urgent, speedy pumps, fucking him just as hard, and they both came. Together.

They rode out the remainder of their dual climax, his hands gliding up her back, and he attempted to draw her to him for a hug.

She wanted to share that post-sex snuggle time with him so much, but resisted every emotional, oxytocin-driven instinct. She had to. "I need to get back to work." And she did, but mostly she needed to guard her heart.

If they continued to have sex — because it could very well be circumstantial, a totally one-off, adrenaline-charged thing — she had to ensure their interactions stayed carnal, casual, devoid of feelings.

Feelings complicated everything, especially with someone like him, who'd happily move onto the next conquest in a heartbeat. As soon as the opportunity arose.

Lexie climbed off Chase, refusing to think too much about the lines of confusion and disappointment on his handsome face. Maybe he wasn't used to women who didn't cling.

Maybe he wasn't used to a woman refusing his request, refusing to want to spend every possible moment with him. Maybe he wasn't used to a woman who behaved how he did. Full stop.

She scurried out of the bedroom, collected her clothes off the corridor floor, and returned to the study. She redressed, logged into her laptop and checked the time. *Almost midday!* Fuck. Time really did fly when having a fabulous fucking time.

But every choice, every action, also had very practical consequences. For each minute of fun, she'd need to match it with the equal amount of work, if she had any chance of continuing to keep him safe, and hopefully solving the crime in conjunction with her specialized team.

A creak, followed by steady footfalls sounded against the timber, coming up the hallway. Shit. She wasn't in the headspace for a deep and meaningful discussion. Lexie stared at her computer screen, pretending to be absorbed with work.

A light knock drew her attention to the door. Chase stood there half naked — unfortunately he'd slipped back into his boxers — leaning his muscular arm against the doorframe and looking totally do-able. She'd already overdosed on him this morning but still wanted more, like an endorphin addict.

She swallowed and tried to look indifferent, unaffected.

"Are you all right?"

Oh no. No! "I'm great, thanks. You?"

She apparently said the right thing because a big, beaming roguish smile replaced his concerned facial expression. Did he think she might regret what had happened? Although it wasn't ideal, she'd enjoyed every single moment, and hoped they could do it again.

As long as they factored in some strict, fuck-for-fun-not-feelings stipulations. She didn't want him to say something, set up for anything, he couldn't follow through with. She'd let him instigate any further sex sessions, and if he didn't, she always had her buzzy buddy to keep her satisfied.

"Fucking best morning I've had in a long time."

She almost drowned in Chase's deep blue gaze. Really? Even though he'd screwed an ever-changing, steady parade of stunning women, even though he could have lost his life?

Either she was a fantastic fuck, or he needed to rethink his lady friends and his overall lifestyle. "Happy to hear it. Happy to hear you've come down from the ledge."

He laughed. Good to know he got her warped sense of humor.

"Um…I need to get back to this. Just don't go out the front. Don't do anything stupid."

A sinful smile spread across his lips. "I'll try my best." He roved his eyes over her, as though he could see beneath her clothes, and he sort of could after viewing her bare body up close and extremely personal not too long ago. "Want something to eat? You must be starving. I know I am."

She tried to subtly squeeze her thighs together. Was he talking about food or sex? Because right now, she could do with both. Desire drove her thoughts, trying to convince her to walk over to him, drop to her knees and suck his dick. She wanted to taste him so badly but she'd said she had too much work to do. So she shouldn't. She really shouldn't.

Her body might crave more of Chase, but her number one priority was to protect the guy. Without that, she'd have no him, no career, and no cock to suck. If she got all her required paperwork done for the day, maybe afterward they could indulge in a repeat performance with a few optional, explorative extras.

Chapter Twelve

"I'd love something for lunch, thank you." She couldn't stop her gaze dropping to his dick and, as quickly as possible, flicked it back to his penetrating eyes.

He flashed her a devilish grin, apparently noticing her wayward glance, and increased the suspense, the teasing, by following what she'd literally requested, and leaving her alone. Dammit. But he'd shown he respected her response, and made the best decision for them both.

Pots and pans clanked, and cupboard doors creaked open and clicked closed providing her with some undisturbed, dedicated work time yet added to her distraction. Which made no sense, given she'd gotten plenty of physical relief not long ago.

Normally after having a series of orgasms, her mind shifted back into gear and she could refocus. But not today, not with him. Today she couldn't get her sexual fix. Couldn't stop her brain from wandering back to Chase and the intimacy they'd shared.

Going by her body's response, she'd gone into some sort of withdrawal. Twitchy, shaking, cravings. Unable to sit still. Obsessive, persistent thoughts. Ridiculous, but factual. She had to divert her mind from going down the fuck-me-again-Chase route.

What was he making? When would it be ready? How soon could she give him head? Not even three thoughts in and she'd already deviated back down the do-him path.

So disturbing. Where was her panty vibrator when she needed it?

"Ready!" Chase called out after who knew how long. She'd become so immersed in thoughts and fantasies she'd lost track of time.

Lexie locked her laptop and met him in the kitchen. On the dining table, he'd placed a homemade hamburger with bacon, cheese, onion, tomato, lettuce and beetroot on a plate with a side of Greek salad. Drink-wise, he'd selected a bottle of sparkling water — her favorite non-alcoholic beverage — and pulled out a chair for her. "Eat up. You need your energy." His voice had that wicked lilt she loved.

Loved? No. Appealed to her lustful needs. Yeah, yeah, that was it.

Chase returned to the kitchen to grab his burger, before she could give him a you're-hilarious, deadpan glare. The man was too quick in so many ways, but thankfully not when it came to sex. That was one place he really took his time, much to their mutual benefit.

He sat opposite and waited until their gazes reconnected. "Want to talk about what happened?"

"No." Lexie stuffed a loose lettuce leaf back into her burger. "Do you?"

"Only if it's going to be a problem."

Her eyebrows pulled together and she stopped fiddling with her food. "If what's going to be a problem?"

"You staying here, working your sexy ass off to protect me."

"Is that all?"

"No." He pushed his untouched plate forward and propped his sinewy forearms on the table. "I want us to continue."

"Continue what, exactly?"

"Sexually interacting. Fucking. Physically appreciating each other. We have a significant spark." He shook his head. "No. It's much more than that. We share an explosive chemistry, an unexpected, unexplainable synergy. And I think we should make the most of it. It's a great, equally enjoyable outlet for both of us."

Exactly the stipulations she'd convinced herself she wanted for them to proceed but, if that was the case, why did she feel so disappointed? She should be overjoyed he'd agreed to more mind-blowing sex, that he wanted to keep things casual, tied to the moment, without deeper meaning. That he wanted to keep within his modus operandi.

Why had she expected anything else? And if he had offered her something more, she'd not have taken him seriously anyway.

Ultimately she'd have had a problem with whatever he'd said. The poor guy couldn't win. *Poor guy, yeah right.* She laughed to herself. At least this way, they could further appreciate each other, have a pleasurable range of activities to engage in while they remained confined indoors.

"Are you good with that?" He searched her eyes as if worried her silence might mean she'd disagree, tell him they could never intimately connect again. Going by both their reactions, it'd be a huge loss for each of them, on a lust level.

"Let's see how we go." As in, she would try it out but if it all got too hard for her, for either of them, she'd call an end to their fuckfest.

"So let me be clear." He held her gaze captive. "I want to touch you, taste you, fuck you. Every day. More than once a day. Is that what you want?"

Fuck yes. "Sounds good." Exciting, exhilarating. "But if either of us asks to stop, for any reason, we need to respect that decision."

"Of course. Consent is essential. I don't want to be intimate with someone who isn't interested."

That would definitely not be the reason she'd ask him to cease their interactions. More like, she'd become *way too* interested. While he hadn't. "Then, we're right to go. Consider this morning's activities the new usual."

"Excellent. Best news I've heard all day. Now eat, or your lunch will get cold."

She took a bite of her burger, his eyes following the swipe of her tongue licking over her lips.

"And when you're done, come over here."

She stopped mid-chew, tingles of awareness spiking in her stomach. What would he request? Maybe she could kneel between his legs and suck his dick for dessert?

They ate the rest of their meals in anticipatory silence, then she collected their plates and loaded them and the remaining dirty dishes in the dishwasher. She turned back to Chase and he sat at the table angled toward her, watching, waiting. Testing to see whether she'd follow through.

She fixed her stare on his breathtaking blue eyes and sauntered toward him, stopping right between his golden-brown legs. For a guy who sat in his office or paraded around in court all day, he was surprisingly tanned.

He had to worship the sun on his days off, or probably went for a jog in nothing but sneakers and skimpy shorts on his lunch break. She hoped he had a snug gray pair. "What now?" Her voice came out all husky, and she struggled to stand still.

"Whatever you want."

"You're up for whatever I decide?"

"Yep."

"So if I said I have a strap-on in my luggage and I want to fuck your ass, you'd be cool with it?" She peered at him, ready for the guy to backtrack.

"With you, yeah. Prostate play makes me come like a fucking fountain. And I trust you'd peg me with passion."

She would. She hadn't done it heaps but she knew how to make the whole experience sexy and fun for both people. Not that she'd have ever considered him a viable, interested candidate. Another unanticipated, positive revelation.

He caressed her cheek. "Is that what you want?"

"Not right now, no." She glanced at the massive bulge in his black boxers, and regained eye contact.

"So what *do* you want? Spell it out for me. I want to hear every explicit word aloud."

Why did she suddenly feel so nervous? Because when she felt confronted she tended to answer with action, bypassing her stammering anxiety. She averted her gaze to her feet and went to talk.

He tilted her chin up. "And look me in the eye when you say it." Chase kept hold of her jaw, not forcefully, but firmly, preventing her from glancing away.

"I...I want dessert."

"What sort of dessert?" He pressed his thumb to her lips, encouraging her to lick it, suck it. And she did. Exactly what she wanted to do to his cock.

He growled, slipping his thumb from her moist mouth and swiping the pad of it across her lips. "Tell me what you want."

"To suck your dick."

"Mmm...I want that too. But first, no clothes. I need to slide my cock between your beautiful breasts."

She whipped everything off, kneeled in front of him, and squeezed her boobs together, guiding his cock to slide within the tight channel she'd created. He thrust into the snug space over and over and over, dropped his head back and grunted.

The moment the pre-cum leaked out, she exposed his erection and licked the head. He smelled and tasted salty, musky, sexy — as divine and addictive as how she'd imagined.

Lexie gripped his shaft and started to pump in time with her licks. His groans grew louder and louder and more frequent, and she sucked the length of him into her mouth.

In the past, she'd dabbled in BDSM and played with a regular Dom who'd taught her the art of deep throating. And she'd perfected it to the point where she could easily bypass her body's natural gag reflex.

Chase weaved his fingers through her hair and tugged, sending a flare of pleasure to her core, and she took him deeper. They got into a rhythm — him fucking her mouth, her rolling and rubbing and stroking his balls — and not even a minute later he came down her throat with a roar.

The tightness of his grip on her head loosened and he slumped back in his seat, his cock slipping from her mouth. She licked her lips and swallowed every last drop of him.

"Fuck, Lexie."

"Is that what you'd like now?" She couldn't stop the proud, smart-ass smirk from forming on her face.

"Yeah, I would, but my dick needs a bit of time to recover." He grasped her hand, jumped up and led her into their shared bedroom. She had no doubt they'd have more sex shortly, but what would happen after? Would he push for them to cuddle? And how would she handle it if he did?

Chase let go of her hand, stepped out of his boxers and lay on his back. "Get on all fours, line up your clit with my mouth and jerk me off gently, while I eat you out. Once you come, and I'm all nice and hard, we'll fuck. How does that sound?"

Fucking fantastic. "It's like you read my thoughts."

He laughed, all sexy and raspy and ready to go. Like her, the man was insatiable. From what she'd seen, and experienced, their sex drive and attraction to one another matched perfectly.

She climbed onto him, and angled her pelvis, pressing her dripping wet pussy in his face. As requested. And he wasted not even a second, licking in and around her folds, tonguing her entrance and rimming her ass.

She grabbed Chase's semi-hard cock, and started to pull him off with soft, light strokes, not wanting him to go numb or painfully oversensitive. "How's that?"

His groan of approval reverberated against her hot flesh. Lexie let his physical and verbal responses guide her, while his talented tongue and fingers took her to the orgasmic brink. She moaned with full abandon.

He stilled her hand and went harder at her pussy. She cried out and came all over his lips, his tongue, his chin, his cock engorged and throbbing in her grip.

"How do you want it?" His voice sounded labored, on-edge and desperate for release. And didn't that drive up her desire to extra turned on.

Staying on all fours, she crawled forward and shifted to the side of him. "From behind."

Chase kneeled between her spread thighs and caressed her ass. "Mmm…my girl likes it doggy style."

His girl? What the hell did that mean? For her, doggy style meant deep, delicious penetration and no eye contact, which equaled less of a chance to blurt out hormone-driven, post-sex sentiments. It helped to appreciate the moment without expecting more. "I love it."

"So do I."

Unsurprising. He wrapped her free-flowing hair around his fist and thrust his dick to the absolute hilt, managing to press every single one of her pleasure points. If she wasn't careful, she'd come again before he even had a chance to move, to draw out his own high-octane orgasm.

"I love your hair loose and wild. So long and silky and sexy," he said, and tugged a little harder. The perfect amount of pressure and bite accelerated her desperation to come, but she wanted to wait for him. "Leave it out like this for me."

Lexie's *sure* sounded more like a moan, and somehow she held off climaxing. His fingers gripped tight to her hip, her hair, and he gave into ecstasy. She followed within moments and they collapsed onto the mattress, both basking in the afterglow and attempting to recover.

If they kept going at it like this, when would she muster the energy to work? How would he? She couldn't deny that getting off helped to refocus but not when it became an obsession or an easily accessible opportunity to escape. They needed to watch for anything that could compromise their overall safety.

"You okay?" Chase lifted the bulk of his weight off her, swept her hair aside and kissed her sweaty nape.

"I am. You?"

"I'm much better than okay. I could go again, but I should let you get back to work."

Go again? So could she. She'd thought the female multiple-orgasm thing, maybe even a nympho thing, played a part in her heightened libido, but given his reply, apparently the concept extended way past her skewed, simplistic, sex-and-sleep view of men. Or so she'd soon see.

Chapter Thirteen

Let Mike out. If you don't, you'll pay.

Don't push me. You'll regret it.

I can't wait much longer. And neither can Mike.

The last three messages in Chase's public messenger app. Should he tell Lexie?
Yeah.
Did he?
No.
Why?
He didn't want to disrupt their new normal. A couple of weeks had gone by where they continued to order groceries online, established a work and fucking schedule, and had no more overt, life-threatening encounters. And no clear list of suspects. Just eating scrumptious food and indulging in amazing sex. Not a bad side benefit. No one would hear him complaining.

He hadn't had the ability to exercise outside but the inside workouts compensated incredibly well.

Oh, and in addition to the food and fucking, their discussions also played a significant part in his overarching level of satisfaction.

Chase made them breakfast, and went to call her. She sat in the study, like she did every day, focused on keeping up to date with any fresh information and discovering any new leads.

With her so engrossed, he stood silent and watched. It might sound a bit strange, creepy, almost stalkerish, but it wasn't. He appreciated beauty, and Lexie epitomized beautiful, inside and out. And she'd kept her shiny, thick black hair free flowing down her back as he'd requested, making him extra hard.

Sexy, considerate, loving...even though she tried to hide it. She hadn't said anything about her reluctance to snuggle with him but it screamed *I've been hurt*. And *I'm not ready, might never be ready, to trust a man again*.

And he respected that. So he wouldn't push her. He too had prioritized freedom so had caged off his heart, and did everything in his power not to get attached. Up until their forced confinement in his cabin, he'd made sure never to spend this much time with any woman who'd shared his bed.

Usually he wanted to move on after a few days, meet someone else, get that exciting, new-relationship-full-of-hot-sex feeling. But his circumstances wouldn't allow it.

Oh, the situation permitted consensual hot sex but not the frequent change in partner. So why didn't he care about seeking out a new woman? A first. What did Lexie have that held his attention, retained his interest, his attraction? Why did the idea of moving on from her bother him?

Had they fallen victim to their own weird, obscure sort of Stockholm Syndrome, or forced-proximity, survival stance on a subconscious level?

No. He couldn't entirely put it down to that. Whether he wanted to admit it or not, they had something different, special. As scary and confronting as that sounded.

He couldn't put his finger on what exactly created their potent, unique dynamic, outside of the unusual circumstances, and wouldn't burden her with an emotional deep dive while she remained so compromised.

She already spent a heap of her time torn between enjoying their interactions, managing her emotions, and making sure she completed the required hours to do her job well enough to keep him safe.

"Chase? Everything okay?"

He jolted out of his head and focused on her concerned slate-green gaze. "Breakfast is ready."

"That's it. Nothing else. You're not keeping anything from me?"

What made her question him right at this particular moment? It was as though his subconscious had given her the key to his safeguarded thoughts.

He swallowed. "No." Yes, but he didn't want to worry her prematurely, particularly regarding their relationship. He could sense that if he talked too much, tried to discuss the depth of their emotions and how that impacted on each of them, she'd run.

She wouldn't leave him unprotected, but she'd get onto Alex ASAP and request a replacement. Although he'd harbored reluctant feelings about her competencies at first, he'd grown to see how much she could offer. Personally. Professionally. In terms of challenging him and encouraging growth.

"I know you know, but I just want to reiterate that it's important to tell me everything, even the smallest detail, the tiniest little change that seems out of place."

"If I notice anything of concern, I'll run it by you." Yeah, he'd chosen his words carefully, on purpose — something he excelled at and for very good reason.

Words had more power than people realized, and he'd quickly learned how to choose them wisely. To ensure they met the required circumstances to facilitate the best outcomes. It might sound clinical but it mostly worked…in his experience.

"Good, because it might help crack the case."

"I understand." And although he wanted that, wanted to go back to his 'normal' life, he stressed about losing her in the process. Could what they'd shared transition into the real world? It was impossible to know until tested.

"Don't hold back because you think you'll burden me unnecessarily. I'd rather know all the info so I can make a more accurate decision about how to best proceed."

Beautiful, sexy and smart. His own triple threat. Reinforcing his current need to deflect. "Come here."

She hesitated, then tentatively walked toward him. He wanted to wrap her in a hug but knew better. Didn't want to prematurely pressure her. Instead, he held her hands and pressed a soft kiss to her forehead.

"What's that for?"

"To show my appreciation of you."

"Oh. Um. Thanks." She tried to pull away, but he kept hold of her hands.

"Don't run off."

She laughed. "I can't, even if I want to."

Technically she could, but she showed way too much reliability, showed way too much integrity to leave him stranded and at risk. Her brain might compartmentalize what they shared as work and sex with no greater bond, however, he didn't doubt she'd stand by him.

Knowing Lexie, even as he had for this limited period, he trusted she'd see everything through, from a professional perspective. In terms of her personal life, he still wasn't sure. But who could ever be sure about another's actions and emotions, who could ever one-hundred-percent be sure of their own?

Any time he tried to form a closer, deeper connection, she became as skittish as a spooked horse. So he'd adjusted his approach to gently breaking her in, getting her used to him and what they could accomplish together.

However, if she remained a wild horse, a brumby, at heart, he might have some small gains, with no guarantees for long-term success. As hard as the idea was to accept, he had to stay mindful or else suffer his own emotional setbacks.

He stroked her cheek, and angled her face, ensuring her eyes met his steadfast stare. "Don't ever think you have no choices. If you need to leave, go. I won't guilt or bully you into staying. I won't ever hold you back."

Her gaze darted to the open door. "We should eat." With a nervous smile, she untangled herself from his grasp and escaped to the kitchen.

His sign to change the subject. And he'd honor her wishes, her needs.

For now.

He entered the unspecified, functional, 'safe zone' and she stood by the toaster, her leg shaking. Four slices of toast popped up—golden, exactly how they both liked their bread—and she placed two on his plate and two on hers.

She glanced at him over her shoulder. "Sit. I've got this." Her love languages, acts-of-service style thank you.

He took his regular seat at the dining table, fully accepting her proffered olive branch, while she loaded up their toast with his cheesy, creamy scrambled eggs. She delivered his meal to him, left hers in front of her usual spot, grabbed a couple of glasses and a bottle of pineapple juice—his favorite—and returned.

She poured them each a drink and sat without saying another word. But the atmosphere didn't feel tense. It felt as though they'd broken through another barrier. A small one, but still significant in terms of fostering a positive, supportive, accepting environment.

Chase drank some juice, and had just started on his second piece of toast, when her utensils clinked on her plate. He glanced up and she met his curious gaze.

"Thanks for cooking. Thanks for doing all that you are to make my job, and our time here, easier."

A devilish smile slid onto his lips. "And more enjoyable." He couldn't resist.

Her cheeks turned that glowing ruby red he loved. "Yes, that too. It all helps."

"It definitely does."

She scoffed the rest of the loaded scrambled eggs on her plate, then had a sip of her drink. "Coffee? Tea?"

"I'm good, thanks. Is there something you want to tell me?"

She almost choked on her next forkful.

"You okay?" He pushed away from the table, ready to jump up and give an upward blow to her back to dislodge any wayward food.

"I'm f—" She coughed, and held up her hand. "Fine."

She didn't seem fine. Maybe her discomfort had stemmed from something more than his earlier admission. Maybe she'd come across a concerning development in the case and wondered how to raise it with him.

They both stayed in their 'safe' zones, and she finished off her drink. "Tell me more about George Ulysses and Damien Bacia."

Chase forced down the last couple of mouthfuls of his meal. "George was done for aggravated assault, and Damien for manslaughter. But you probably know that. They've been back in the community for a few weeks now. Have they done anything to arouse your suspicions?"

"No. I just want to make sure I can totally rule them out. Anything else of interest regarding them or their trials?"

"When they were convicted, they both threatened to harm me once they got released."

Her eyes went wide. "So do you think they might have befriended Mike on the inside? Could have made a pact to get you back?" She studied him and gulped as though swallowing something with sharp, jagged edges. "According to all of them, you ruined their lives. And these two have motive and opportunity."

He nursed his remaining half a glass of juice. "Maybe. Possibly. But my gut says it's someone separate, linked directly to Mike DeSalvo outside of prison. Although George and Damien threatened me back then, now that they're out, I don't think they'd jeopardize their freedom. Definitely not for a serial rapist."

Her curious gaze pierced his eyes. "Why?" She pushed her empty plate aside and propped her elbows on the table.

"There's a jail hierarchy. And I know those two considered guys weak if they had to rape women."

"It's not quite that simple. Rape is about power and control."

"I know that, you know that, but not everyone does. Not everyone cares. People have all sorts of prejudices, and can be ignorant and opinionated, and make excuses without full understanding or facts. Not that rape is ever acceptable. Or murder or assault or any crime."

"I agree." Her stare shifted internally, as though reviewing and weighing up what he'd said.

Lexie refocused her curious gray-green gaze on him. "So, if it's not them, who else could possibly support him on the outside? I've searched and searched and haven't been able to find anything on close family or friends. No recorded phone calls or visitors. No physical letters. Mike sounds like a total loner."

"An angry, abusive loner, who took out his frustrations and need for control on vulnerable, defenseless women." Chase tunneled his fingers through his hair. "He had to have made contact with someone, somehow. He probably used some encrypted email address through one of those anonymity-focused providers."

"So you still believe he's one-hundred percent behind this?"

"If not one-hundred percent, bloody close. I'm certain there's some association we're missing."

She fixed her eyes onto his with unblinking determination. "If there is, I'll find it. Or if not me, Alex."

"I know. I trust him and I trust you."

She smiled, apparently appreciating his admiration. "Um…when did you last check the mail?"

Nice deflection. "Here or at home?"

"Both."

"Bills, bills and more bills, going by the police house-sitter feedback at my regular residence. As for here, I haven't set foot outside the front door since the shooting incident." And even then, he hadn't had a chance to collect any letters.

By her expression, although she'd factored in regular sweeps of the property, she hadn't ventured out to the mailbox either. "Let me go and have a look." She said it like she expected someone had left their threatening calling card.

He fucking hoped she was wrong…unless the perp had fucked up and left some evidence to incriminate themselves.

Lexie snapped on some gloves and walked to the door. He followed, and she stopped and turned to him. "Stay right here."

Conflict raged inside him like a tug-o-war. He wanted to abide by her request but couldn't forgive himself if something happened to her. "I recently received more comments on my messenger app."

"What?"

"Same stuff, so I didn't bother saying anything."

"Show me."

He did, and she shook her head and huffed.

"You need to tell me everything. How many times do I need to say that? It all matters."

"Fine. Sorry."

She handed over his phone, grasped the door handle and shot a death glare over her shoulder. "Forward those messages to Alex, and don't even think about coming out here. If anything happens, phone him, then the ambulance. You'll be of no use if we're both injured and unable to call."

Lexie was one-hundred percent right, so he did what she asked, but under his own emotional protest. He needed to get his head around his issue, not her.

Although she hated jogging, she practically sprinted to the mailbox and back, a stack of envelopes in her hand.

The second she stepped inside, he shut and locked the door.

She strode past him and dumped the letters on his dining table.

Bill.

Bill.

Bill.

Tradie advertisement.

Bill.

Local government postal vote forms.

Handwritten envelope with no return address and no stamp.

"Don't touch it." Lexie carefully peeled open the back flap.

She reached inside and extracted a piece of folded white paper. She glanced at him, as though seeking his permission to reveal the contents.

"Go for it. We need to see what it says."

Chapter Fourteen

Lexie unfolded the note, the script written in neat, block letters, dated two days ago. "I'll read it out," she said, but his eager eyes couldn't help but race ahead.

For a smart man like you, I'm surprised you haven't gotten the message. How much clearer do I need to be before you understand? You have no problems pulling all the information together to put people away. What's the difference here? Or are you too distracted by your girlfriend?

I'll make this easy for you. Let me spell it out nice and clear. LET. MIKE. OUT. He doesn't deserve to be behind bars. I know. I'm certain you do too. He's had a rough life. He deserves to be free for once. He deserves to have the opportunity to thrive.

I'll give you a week to let him go. If you don't, you'll know about it. Maybe if something happens to your pretty little goth girlfriend, you might take me seriously.

Fuck. Fuck no. Protecting him was one thing but, just as he'd feared, now he'd added her into the guy's line of fire. "Fuck!" He shoved his hands through his hair and started pacing.

She placed the letter on the dining table, discarded the gloves and touched his arm. He stopped and searched her eyes. How could she look so cool, so calm, so unruffled. "Don't stress."

"I can't help it. I can handle me as a target, but not you. It'd torture me forever if you or anyone I care about got harmed."

Lexie wrapped her arms around his waist and cuddled him close. Their first proper, conscious hug, instigated by Ms. Commitment-phobe. He couldn't talk. Usually he was the one who avoided anything deeper than sex, avoided true intimacy. Though, he had tried with her previously and she'd rejected his advances.

"You're actually a sweet guy." She buried her head in his chest, her voice reverberating with absolute surprise. And an apparently one-hundred-and-eighty-degree change of heart.

He hadn't anticipated her admission, and neither had she, going by her affectionate body language and tone. Sure they'd had a sexual connection, but hadn't exactly clicked personality-wise. In fact, her early responses suggested she'd considered him an unreliable, self-absorbed dick.

She pressed a kiss to his breastbone. So unexpected, so tender, so nice. "We'll keep doing what we're doing. Stay put. Not change anything without thorough consideration. We can't afford to be complacent, make dangerous, flippant, risky decisions. Between Alex and the team, and you and me, we'll work this out. Ensuring everyone's safety is our number one goal."

Chase pressed his palm to her back, and with his other hand, stroked her hair. He admired her assurance, appreciated her dependability and strength, her dedication to her job, to him, and would work with her the best he could to make sure they all remained unharmed.

But broader than that, he wanted her to like him. As a person, not as part of the excitement of her first case. Not simply as a fun, short-term, sexual diversion.

Crazy. Even for him. Normally he utilized any reason to move on, relationship-wise. Though, he'd never been in this exact position. Never had his life on the line. That made a difference, but did it set up for a sustainable way of thinking? Once the threat no longer remained, would he revert to his old beliefs and behavior? Would she?

Lexie's phone rang. "I need to get this."

She broke out of their embrace and ran to the study, most likely to check whether it was Alex or someone else from the Solve Security team. He followed, eager to keep updated on the latest developments. It had an impact on the behavior of both of them.

Chase would do whatever it took to steer clear of adversity, but under her guidance. He'd learned from his previous, gung-ho mistakes. He understood the need to carefully expose the perpetrator as soon as safely possible to extinguish the threat.

It was a fine balance, an intricate dance to achieve the required equilibrium. Like him and Lexie. They had the perfect physical exchange. They aligned in more ways than he'd initially anticipated.

"Alex? Hi," she said, and beckoned Chase into the study. She put his best mate on speaker phone.

"Is Chase there?"

"Yeah, I'm here."

"How are things going?" Alex said, as though he'd sensed something was wrong.

With Lexie, fantastic, with the rest of his life, not so great.

"The perp left a letter in the mailbox. I'll read it to you. Hang on." She raced from the room, and returned with fresh gloves and the letter in hand. With a slow, clear, steady voice, she spoke each chilling sentence aloud, then placed the note on the desk and threw the gloves in the small bin beside her feet.

"That's worrying but it narrows down who could be behind this. And that's a good thing."

Hearing the contents of the note again had Chase retreating into his own little stressed world, while he tried to come to terms with the fact that the suspect knew where he lived. At home, at his alpine retreat. Knew too much about him and Lexie. Knew a hell of a fucking lot about Mike.

The person had awareness of all their movements, had a lifestyle that allowed that level of flexibility. He could, right this moment, have an eye on Chase's cabin and be hatching a plan to break in and hurt him — hurt Lexie — to get the result he required.

Freeing Mike.

Chase wanted to prevent injury, possible death, to himself and others but no way could he let a guy like Mike DeSalvo go free. Not after all the shocking crimes he'd committed, how many women and families and communities he'd terrorized.

The victims who'd survived his attacks would always look over their shoulder, never feel safe. Never feel fully relaxed anywhere. And he couldn't put them or other females at risk.

From his experience, the smart criminals learned and perfected their crimes. Became better at what they did, harder to catch. And no one could afford that, no one wanted some super-skilled, aggressive rapist lurking around their neighborhood.

"Although no distinctive DNA evidence came back on the rock and taped note, post me this new letter in its envelope and I'll organize for thorough fingerprint and genetic testing. I know it's a longshot but sometimes people make stupid mistakes," Alex said, his no-nonsense tone firm.

"I'm not sure I should leave Chase alone. The assailant knows where he is, that I'm here with him. If they see me go into town—"

"There's no way around this. Be as quick as you can. And, Chase, you need to lock all the doors and windows and stay inside. Don't let anyone in except Lexie. Got me?"

Fuck that. "No. You're not sending her alone, not after the guy's threatened both of us." What if he assaulted her? Splitting them up was probably what the attacker had hoped for. A very positive byproduct. It gave him easier access to either, possibly both of them. And whether he targeted Lexie or him, Chase would be equally devastated.

"Sorry, mate, but there's no other way. I need to get that letter to the lab ASAP. Lexie can look after herself. It's you I'm worried about."

Alex had fucking jammed him into an inescapable corner. He gritted his teeth. "Sounds like I don't have a say."

"In this instance, you don't. I know you're not used to that, but unfortunately we don't always have control. We don't always get what we want, what we think is right." Alex's voice virtually punched him in the gut.

Lexie stared at him, her eyes filled with a loving appreciation. For him, as a whole, for the difficulty they both faced, or for his consideration of her wellbeing? "I'll be fine."

Would she? He fucking hoped so. But like she'd reinforced to him before—and if he had any chance of retaining her romantic interest—he had to show he trusted her and her abilities. "Do what you have to do and hurry back. And while you're gone, I'll stay locked inside. I won't do anything risky."

"You won't do anything but what I tell you. And if you notice something odd, concerning, out of place, you ring me and Lexie."

"I understand." He'd learned his it-didn't-work-to-hold-back-info lesson. No matter how much his subjective mind tried to convince him that was the best decision.

"Do you? Because Lexie mentioned your little hero routine the other week. You need to trust her, and me. Do you think I'd have assigned someone that I didn't believe could do the job?"

Oh, that too. Yeah. He needed to also curb his fear-driven responses. "Of course not."

"Then stop trying to be a savior. Stop trying to prove your masculinity. Or you'll get yourself or Lexie or both of you hurt, possibly killed. You'll undo all the good work, all the effort we've put in to protect you. You need to let go of that fucking ego."

So Alex. Chase considered this guy his best mate for a reason. Alex never held back, had always spoken in a blunt, honest, straight-up way with him. "So, what are you saying? You need to be a bit clearer." Chase chuckled. He had to make light of the situation or dread would set in like a cold permeating frost, which could put him and Lexie in extra danger.

"This is serious, mate."

Chase sobered. "I know." Too fucking serious.

"Good. Then promise me you'll listen to us."

Alex's military background meant he had plenty of experience with fighting enemies, totally outshone Chase in that area, so he had to respect his best friend's opinion. "I promise."

"Okay, Lexie, good luck. Keep me updated. Any questions from either of you, you know how to reach me."

"Thanks, Alex." She raised her eyebrows at Chase as if to say, 'don't cause any more trouble'.

"And, Chase, you behave." His mate warned him again, like he could see Lexie's concerns, plus he knew what Chase was capable of — stretching the rules. Not to sound up himself, but Chase had recognized early on that he excelled at making a square peg fit beautifully in the roundest of holes.

Alex, and apparently Lexie, knew him a bit too well. "Yes, sir." He'd do his best to rein in his knight-charging-in-on-a-white-horse complex.

"Fucking smart ass." Alex's disgruntled voice couldn't conceal his signature smile. Not that Chase could see him, but he knew his mate inside out and back-to-front. They'd known each other too long to successfully hide any secrets. Even if they tried. "Keep him in line, Lexie."

"I will." Her penetrating, unblinking eyes stayed fixed on Chase's face.

"And make sure you inform me of any new developments."

"We will. You too." Lexie hung up, her stare never wavering. "I hope you're going to do what he says."

"Within justifiable bounds."

"What does that mean?" She squinted her gorgeous slate-green, super-suspicious eyes at him.

He strode over to Lexie and wrapped her in his arms. "I'll do whatever it takes to support you and keep us both safe."

"No hero stuff, right? You won't overstep."

"Not when it comes to our safety, no. But I will if it comes to your pleasure."

She studied his eyes as though silently scrutinizing his reasoning, as if she was the fairness police.

He held her face between his hands. "With consent. Always with your consent."

An appreciative smile stretched across her sensual, full lips. Lips he loved on his mouth, his nipples, his cock. Anywhere on his body. She excelled at activating all his sexual buttons.

"So now that we're clear, I need to post that note to Alex." She broke away from Chase, leaving a cold, empty space, a palpable gut-wrenching gap.

He really didn't want her traveling into town on her own, but he needed to let go, as Alex reinforced. He needed to trust in her skills and Alex's judgment. But emotions were the opposite of rational.

They infiltrated the mind, and reduced the ability to think clearly, clouding any attempt at an accurate assessment of actions and events. They had a tendency to create doubt and turmoil and conflict.

"Send the letter, then get back here as soon as you can. No fluffing around."

"I don't fluff. That's your forte."

"Excuse me?" He blinked at her and slammed his hand on his heart, feigning offence.

Her smile radiated with triumph. "Who was the one that hung back and chatted to locals, delaying our departure out of town when we arrived?"

"I explained that it would look more suspicious if I ignored them and rushed off."

She rolled her eyes. "Right. You could have acknowledged them, said a quick hello and mentioned you'd catch up soon."

"I could have... I know what to do next time. We're always living and learning, aren't we?"

"If we choose to." She pressed a palm to his chest and the other onto his hip. "You sure you don't want a coffee from your friend's café?"

Was that a test? "No. I want you back as soon as possible." He dove down for a kiss, hoping to highlight without words, the need for her to be careful, and to reinforce how much he cared.

When they pulled away, she stumbled, her eyes dazed, mirroring exactly how he felt. *Fuck, this woman...*

"I need to get a plastic bag —"

"Wait. I'll grab a Ziploc." Chase strode straight to the kitchen cupboard selected the suitable size plastic sleeve and a box of latex-free gloves, then returned to the study.

She donned a fresh pair of gloves, then slipped the note into the plastic storage bag and sealed it. "Thanks."

"Thank *you*."

Lexie pressed a quick goodbye kiss to his lips, and tucked the Ziploc into her huge handbag, jumped into the car and took off into town.

Chapter Fifteen

Lexie parked in the tree-lined street, a couple hundred meters from the post office, the foliage a spectacular blend of red, amber, green and purple. Although she'd always preferred black to bright colors, something about autumn spoke to her soul.

Maybe it was the beauty of decay, death, transition and rejuvenation. Not a typically pretty subject, but her experience showed that cycles happened and formed the foundation of life. How each person connected with the series of phases made the difference.

Did they acknowledge them or do everything to avoid their existence? Do anything to avoid recognizing message repetition, ignore the need for change? Positive or negative.

A tradie dressed in long dark shorts and a high-vis vest swept fallen leaves from the nature strip into bags. She'd never understood why people raked the gorgeous, confetti-style sprinkling that piled up at the foot of tree trunks. Aside from adding to the beauty, the composting process had significant benefits on the soil...from what Chase had explained.

Chase. She sighed. Who'd have pegged him as a nature type? Not her. He'd consistently come across as a full-on city, urban-lifestyle guy, reinforcing the importance of not judging an unknown book by its superficial cover.

Not that his cover didn't tick all her extremely appealing boxes — he could feature on one of those romance novels her friends read — but his outward appearance couldn't and wouldn't hold her attention. Physical attractiveness faded. She needed depth, and he'd demonstrated a surprising amount of it.

Lexie grabbed her bag off the passenger seat and undertook a thorough visual scan of the environment. Quiet. Sleepy. Except for the tradie-gardener, and a scattering of parked cars.

Ideal, or was it? Maybe the lack of people, the absence of potential witnesses increased the assailant's access to her, to Chase.

No catastrophizing.

She stepped out onto the bitumen, locked the car and stood tall and confident. She couldn't let her mind lead her down a precarious, unsubstantiated path. Fear could make a person choose poorly. And she couldn't allow that. She needed to be on form, do her job, and get back ASAP to protect Chase.

Lexie did another quick sweep of her surroundings, threw her keys in her bag, and undertook a brisk short walk to the post office. Out the front, she disposed of her discarded gloves in the rubbish bin, then stepped inside.

She selected and wrote on a suitably sized express-post envelope, addressing the contents *care of Alexander*

Barrett at Solve Security, and stood in the queue, constantly evaluating everyone and everything around her, as subtly as possible.

A thirty-something mother with a snoozing baby in a pram, an elderly man with a walker, and a policeman with his radio crackling. No one looked suss, but that didn't cross them off the suspect list. Until she and her team could narrow down the pool of people, any locals, in particular, could feasibly fit the criteria.

A few minutes later she reached the top of the line and handed the express package to a customer service rep. "I need this sent as urgently as possible, to an address in Melbourne, Victoria, please."

"No problem. It should arrive by tomorrow."

All she could do was pay and hope for the best.

On the way out she scoured the street, the black sky looming overhead. Someone touched her forearm and she tried not to flinch at the unexpected contact.

"Lexie? How's Chase?"

She glanced up into a familiar-ish face. "Um…fine. Thank you." She needed to be careful what she disclosed. Unfortunately, unless ruled out by evidence, no one was exempt from consideration in Chase's case.

He studied her eyes, as though checking for her recognition. "Jimmy. We met a few weeks ago. I own the local café, near the supermarket."

"Oh. Yes. Hi." She forced a sociable, friendly smile. "Chase is enjoying his well-overdue holiday."

"That's great. Is he not with you?" Jimmy looked past her, to Chase's car, then up and down the road, as though expecting him to appear.

"Not today."

"Oh. That's a shame. I'd hoped to see him, arrange a proper catch up. When he came into the café, he was, well, not himself. I wanted to make sure he was okay."

A bit persistent, but maybe it indicated he actually cared? "He is, thank you." She fiddled with her keys, trying to send the message that she needed to go.

"Sounds like he really deserved the time away."

She forced a smile, eager to shutdown the conversation as quickly and pleasantly as possible and return home. No, not home—Chase's cabin. "He did, he does. I'll let him know you asked after him," she said, and hurried toward Chase's car.

Not even a couple hundred meters later a man's voice commandeered her attention. "Lexie? Am I right?"

Another recognizable person approached her. *Fuck.* At this rate, she wouldn't make it back to Chase for hours. Apparently 'coming into town' and 'quick trip' were mutually exclusive terms.

The guy blocked her path along the sidewalk just before she reached the car. "Hi?" She held her handbag close to her hip, keys in hand, ready, if need be, to use either as a weapon.

His smile looked sincerely cheerful, harmless. But that could also be the sign of a master psychopath. "You probably don't remember me, but I didn't expect you to. I'm the supermarket owner, Dan. Chase has known me for years."

"I do remember." Now. As soon as he clarified the missing pieces, her memory fell into place. "I'll let him know you said hello."

"Thank you." Like Jimmy, he looked around—scouring the street as though expecting to see Chase—his eyebrows pulled together.

Such busybodies! No wonder she'd stayed in the city—no one cared what anyone did. Everyone kept to themselves and minded their own, very private business.

The idea of someone or several people keeping tabs on her gave her the creeps. Though, it could be helpful for law enforcement when something went wrong.

"Why isn't he with you? Normally he loves coming into town when he visits."

A little bit too interested? Or maybe legitimately concerned? She should run the interactions with Jimmy and Dan past Chase, get his opinion about what had transpired, once she made it back to his cabin.

At least she hoped to make it back to him unscathed, and soon, given Chase's car was within touching distance. "He's having some down time, recuperating from an awfully busy year. So, I'm his girl Friday for a little while."

His conspiratorial smile suggested he assumed Chase had hidden himself away with a woman for some covert adult fun, a dirty few weeks, if nothing else. Some hands-on, extremely enjoyable physical therapy without the sticky-beak community talking.

Except her experience today suggested people who knew him loved sticking their noses in, enjoyed gossip, sought answers. They all had their theories and wanted them proven right.

"Lucky man. If I were him, I'd extend things as long as possible."

Lexie didn't disagree. She loved it when Chase extended his thing as long as possible. "Awww...thank you. I'll let Chase know you asked about him." She smiled, stepped onto the road, opened the driver's side door and sunk into the seat, pressing the key fob to lock the car. No one else milled around but anyone could show up without warning, going by her recent ambush.

She started the engine, the sky dense with gray clouds, the tiniest sliver of sunlight escaping through a slit in the darkness. Her stomach twisted into a tight, tangled knot. Why? The conversations she'd had with the two men hadn't shown any hint of red flags, didn't ring any blaring alarm bells, so how come she felt so uneasy?

Maybe being away from Chase? Maybe the whole situation had started to take its emotional, exhausting toll. Maybe her previous police work and new protection role had skewed her view.

Her lack of findings far from proved their innocence. Maybe they excelled at hiding their crimes. Only time, and further digging, would tell. Sadly, until she had more evidence and a clear motive, she needed to treat everyone with strict scrutiny.

It took the whole drive to settle her stomach. Eager to reunite with Chase, she parked in the garage, tingles of excitement shooting up her spine, and power-walked up the front path. Before she could even reach out to grab the handle, he whipped the door open and practically yanked her inside.

"What are you doing?" He slammed the door shut and held her to him like he never wanted to let her go. And didn't that fucking screw with her already endangered heart.

His eyes darted to the window behind her as though searching the surroundings for possible threats. She didn't blame him for his paranoia, but he needed to scale down his stress a peg or twenty. Hypervigilance had a tendency to create more assumptions, more fear, more issues.

Yes, they'd had scary moments, yes, an active threat remained, but with the support of Solve Security, Lexie had it under control. To this point. "Returning ASAP, as per your request."

"I appreciate that, but don't dawdle outside."

"Dawdle?" She shrugged out of his embrace and peered into his eyes. She'd practically sprinted up the path and he knew she hated running. But stressed minds saw what they wanted to see, what confirmed their pre-existing, fearful biases.

"Last time we were only out of the cabin for five minutes and…" He ran both hands through his hair. "You're a target too. Whoever it is thinks you're my girlfriend so they might want to hurt you to hurt me."

"And what do *you* think? What exactly am I to you?"

He scrubbed a hand over his bristled jaw, his cheeks turning an embarrassed, *gotcha* red. "My bodyguard, my lover, hopefully my friend."

"Right." She knew it, knew she should keep her heart distant, try not to get emotionally involved. But rational minds rarely agreed with feelings and often got overridden.

Of course he'd never take her seriously. How could she have started to believe he would? Wanting to cuddle didn't confirm anything other than he enjoyed close body contact.

Chase could say all the sweetest words in the world but ultimately she didn't fit his model-girlfriend, stunning-woman, arm-candy mold. Didn't fit his long-term relationship 'standards'. Only his temporary, disposable, convenient-fuck criteria.

Just like her fucking ex-fiancé. Why did she keep attracting the same sort of men? She must take some perverse pleasure in self-flagellation, have low self-confidence, or feared commitment. Maybe all three. Maybe she mirrored these men's behavior in her own way? Self-sabotaged.

There was no time to dig through her maze of unresolved issues. Right now she had to do her role. At least she knew where she honestly stood.

His steadfast, affectionate attention had broken through her protective emotional wall, ripped apart her safety net, and made her think she might mean more. But apparently not. He probably treated every momentary woman the same way. Lulled them into believing he actually cared beyond sex.

"I didn't think you wanted anything deeper." Sincere surprise tinged his tone.

Or maybe he'd perfected his I-respect-you-and-your-wishes response. A way to considerately deflect blame. "And if I did?"

"You haven't shown it."

So? What the fuck did that mean? If he saw a romantic future between them, what had stopped him from asking her opinion, her stance, from seeking clarity rather than assuming?

More deflection, more distraction, less taking responsibility. He'd still avoided answering her question. Would he be interested? Wouldn't he? Chase expected her to commit to a reply, so why couldn't he? Why couldn't he take initiative, lead by the required example? Give her some sense of his expectations.

Tears burned the back of her eyes like acid. Fuck, she'd promised herself she wouldn't fall for his charming bullshit. "Neither have you," she spat back.

Not entirely true—his actions had shown maybe he did see her as someone more serious. Obviously it reflected her hopes, not reality. She shook her head. "Anyway, whatever. I'm here to do a job."

"What d-does that mean?" His voice staggered, like her words had stabbed him in the heart, his tone laced with defensiveness and disappointment.

"That I'll do everything I can to protect you. I'll do everything to solve this case, to get the assailant apprehended. That's it." As in, no more intimate interactions, no more touching, no more sex. She couldn't keep going as they were or she'd struggle to dig herself out of the deepening, heartbreaking hole.

First and irrefutably foremost, she couldn't continue to hide behind the casual hook-up lifestyle and pretend it was good enough. Knowing Chase had reinforced she couldn't return to that and stay happy. He'd taught her she needed a man in her life who valued her in her entirety, that she could no longer settle for anything else.

Lexie took off before he could say all the right things and wrangle his way back into her highly compromised good books, and locked herself in the study. If he were smart, he'd leave her alone.

She slumped into his office chair, slotted her headphones into place, and unlocked the computer. She scrolled through email after email.

Nothing new.

Minutes passed, an hour, two hours, more, and not even a glimpse of him. He'd honored her silent but regretful 'do-not-disturb' sign. She flicked on the desk lamp and tried to redirect her energy into reviewing the evidence, doing a deep dive into people's motives, yet still couldn't come up with a culprit.

Lexie hit dead-end after dead-end. Nothing seemed to work for her today. She'd fallen out of alignment with the environment. Or at least, that's what her new-age brother would say.

Fucking frustrating. Fucking infuriating. Fucking typical.

She dropped her head into her hands and blew out a breath in an attempt to reset herself and refocus her energy.

A couple of minutes later, she fixated on her computer screen, reread all the info Alex had sent through—for the millionth time, hoping she'd notice something different, something that stood out—but still couldn't find a connection.

She had to keep plugging away, they all did. Her, Alex, Chase, the team. They needed to keep on top of new findings and regularly reassess existing information, to help determine who, other than Mike or someone connected to him, would gain from this barrage of threats.

A knock sounded on the door. "Lexie?"

She glanced at the time on the bottom corner of the computer monitor. Close to eight p.m. With the lamp's persistent glow, and her swearing off giving Chase any more consideration outside of the case, she hadn't realized so many hours had passed. "Go watch some TV or go to bed. I have a lot to work through." And even if she didn't, she'd find something.

"You still need to eat, and sleep."

She did, but she couldn't sit or lie beside him, a man who didn't take her seriously. A man whose touch her body still craved…to her detriment. "I can eat and sleep here."

"Please don't do this."

Don't shut him out? Don't close down his one and only avenue for in-person conversation? Don't shut off the sex-on-tap? She yanked off her headphones and slammed them onto the desk. "Do what? Look after myself?"

He breathed out a loud breath. "Can I please open the door? I need to see you."

She hesitated, letting him stew for a few seconds to ensure he didn't get too overconfident and cocky. "Fine." She kept her eyes focused on the screen, relying on her peripheral vision.

Chase cracked open the door wide enough to peer inside. He stared at her so hard, she could partially see but mostly feel his eyes boring into her face, pleading, desperate for her positive acknowledgment, her attention. "Lexie, I miss you. I want you." He stepped inside the room.

"Stay where you are." She held up her hand but still didn't look directly at him. And to his credit, he didn't come closer. "I want you too, but physical desire isn't enough. I need more."

"So do I."

She shot her gaze to him. "Prove it."

"How?" He shifted on the spot and shoved his hands through his hair with palpable exasperation.

"You're a smart guy. I'm sure you can think of something."

He heaved out a heavy breath and met her don't-screw-with-me gaze. "Look, I'm sorry about before. Your question took me by surprise. I wasn't prepared. I didn't express myself clearly, accurately."

"It sounded clearer than clear to me. Aren't you normally the king of clarity? Mr. Articulate, Mr. Amazing-with-words, Mr. Verbal-gymnastics."

"In certain circumstances. Definitely when it comes to work. That's my forte. My daily bread and creamy butter. But even then, I do a shit-ton of planning and make sure I understand my subject as well as possible, rehearse my speech and questions until I know them back-to-fucking-front.

"In my private life...fuck... I don't get the information beforehand, I don't get the opportunity to put together a plan and practice. I get tongue-tied, don't say the right things around beautiful women, women I'm attracted to, women who I desperately want to like me."

"You?" She couldn't have heard right. Had someone kidnapped the real Chase and put this man in his place? "You're worried about women liking you? Who fucking doesn't? If I did a survey, I'd estimate nearly ninety-five percent of females would do you in a heartbeat."

He laughed, his eyes crinkling at the corners. "Thank you. And maybe you're right. But they want me for my outer shell, my reputation, my status. I'm sick of that. I don't just want any pretty, interested woman."

"Who do you want?"

"Fuck. Fuck me." He shook his head, took a breath and strode right up to her, his eyes penetrating her soul. "You."

Really? She found that almost impossible to believe. "For now. While it suits the circumstances."

"No." He held her face, making sure she couldn't look away. "I mean it. Yes, I've got a reputation as a player, but it's not me. I don't enjoy it. I did at the start, but not anymore. Fuck, every straight guy's dream is to fuck a range of beautiful women. But it gets boring, unsatisfying.

"I've probably gone about things the wrong way, made everything harder for myself but being with you has highlighted the importance of clicking with a woman across the board, has provided a compelling argument for entering into something that has a greater chance of longevity, sustainability."

Sounded enticing, promising but... "Why do you think that person might be me?"

"You're smart, you're beautiful, you challenge me in a positive way. You get my work and the associated long hours and accompanying stresses. You've made me rethink things, my limited views, my beliefs, my restricted perspective. And our chemistry is mind melting, earth shattering."

Chase kept his magnificent eyes on hers the whole time, making it significantly harder for him to successfully lie and manipulate. He prided himself on not leading women on, on straight-up honesty. Now she had the chance to test his proclamation firsthand. "You really are great with words."

"I'm not bullshitting you. I'm expressing myself as clearly as I can."

"So, what does that mean? When the situation changes, you might change your mind?"

"No. Fuck, you really don't trust me." His eyes turned glassy, like ice melting across the top of a frozen lake. No fake crying crap—any con person could master that—this was heartfelt. Amazingly. Unexpectedly.

"I want to. You seem legitimate, but my ex-fiancé did too."

"Ex-fiancé? What the fuck?" He searched her eyes and stroked her cheek with the pad of his thumb. "What happened?"

"Grab a seat." She locked the computer and Chase positioned a chair beside her. He sat and clasped her hand, silent, patient, encouraging. The soft warm glow of the desk lamp enhanced his features, highlighting his concern.

In so many ways, over the last few days, Chase had backed her growing belief that severing ties with her ex was a blessing. Not that she was religious, but she got the gist.

A rush of unexpressed words welled up inside her, ready to erupt. Fuck. Outside of completing a statement for her previous workplace, she hadn't told anyone this story, other than Alex. And even then, she'd given him the absolute abridged version.

She'd mostly let the traumatizing memories roll around and around in her head, trying to view them from every possible angle and see whether she'd missed anything. Whether she was more culpable.

Could she have done something better? Should she have handled things differently? Because for all the distress he'd caused, all the accusations and lack of support, she realized her actions played a part, she still had to acknowledge some fault. What would Chase say, when she told him the full details?

"I'm not sure how much you know about me."

"Only that you were injured while working a job."

Guilt kicked her in the solar plexus. "A job I wasn't supposed to do."

"Oh. They're always the ones that get you." He squeezed her hand between his big, warm comforting palms. "Tell me what happened."

Chapter Sixteen

Lexie could have drowned in the depths of his blue eyes. Intent, intrigued, interested, without a hint of harsh judgment. Unlike anyone she'd ever known. "We'd tracked down possible leads for ages and finally got confirmation on a suspect.

"As lead detective, I'd put so much time and effort into the police investigation, I wanted to be there for the arrest. And I was, but the prick took a couple of shots at us before he got apprehended, and unfortunately I took the brunt of it." She went into every explicit detail and he listened, his eyes focused on her the whole time.

"Thank fuck you survived." He lifted the back of her hand to his lips and pressed a lingering kiss to her skin. "What was your fiancé's response?"

She averted her gaze, trying to distance herself from the events that annoyingly, still scarred her, created an invisible yet equally deep wound. "My boss, at the time, notified him, but he didn't come to the hospital. Instead, he broke off our relationship via text."

"What?" Chase jolted up, his back stiff and straight, as though disbelieving the guy's reaction.

"I'd pissed him off once too often. I was supposed to attend our engagement dinner but prioritized a job." She broke away from Chase and buried her face in her hands. Would he back her fiancé's decision? Saying the circumstances aloud made her question her own choices.

"So, let me get this right. He didn't check if you were okay, and his overall behavior and lack of tact essentially added to your pain."

She met his concerned stare. "It did. But he got so caught up in his own hurt and disappointment, I think part of him needed to upset me in retaliation."

Chase shook his head and sighed. "Well, that's just fucking bullshit. You were his wounded fiancée, for fuck's sake. An inpatient in hospital. He bailed at the biggest crisis you'd had to face as a couple. It's probably hard to hear, but he did you a huge favor. He didn't deserve you.

"Anyone who really knows you, can see how much you love your work, love seeking justice. That you want the best for everyone, and sometimes that takes precedence over yourself, over your private life. That other less pressing things can wait. It makes a difference to a heap of people. And I get that."

"You do?" Her hope-filled gaze latched onto him.

"More than you know. However, many don't understand, for various reasons—beliefs, values, experience. It's the other main motive for why women don't stick around.

"I've lost count of how many times I've had people tell me I'm married to my job. And I suppose I am. I have been, but this eventuation has made me re-evaluate things. I still love my work, aim to achieve the best outcomes, though it's reinforced that, if I survive, maybe I can do things differently. Better."

Lexie looped her arms around him, his soothing, arousing heat seeping into her. "You're going to survive. And you know what? I'll do whatever it takes to keep you connected to what you love."

"I know you will. And I intend to do the same for you." He held her tighter. "I really, really hope I make it out of here so I can further explore our relationship."

Did he get what that actually entailed? "As long as you understand —"

"That you and me might sometimes need to work when we're not supposed to."

She smiled, relief surging through her. The perfect answer. "Exactly. Sounds like we both get what it's going to take."

"It does. But just so you know, I plan to have a quiet word with your boss."

She smacked Chase's arm. "You will not."

"Of course I will. I understand you needing to see a job through, but I don't want you harmed."

"That's very sweet, but my work will put me in danger at times, as we've spoken about. There's no avoiding the reality of it. I'd happily sign up for simpler jobs, but sometimes they're the ones that go rogue. It's impossible to know what's simmering below the superficial surface. Things are often more complex than they appear. But I'm sure you're aware of that. With security and protection comes risk."

He exhaled and kissed the top of her forehead. "I know. I don't like it because I care about you, but I accept and respect your choices. I trust you and your expertise, as well as Alex's judgment.

"I trust that you and your team will ensure you're as safe as possible. And, so we're clear, I'd never hold it against you if something didn't go to plan. I'd be right beside you, supporting you all the way."

She wanted to have faith in what he said but did he really mean every word? Could he truly stand by her when it mattered? Should she give him the chance to show whether his actions matched what he promised? "I want to believe what you're saying—"

"But?"

"My fiancé said all the right things too, was an expert at lip service. How do I know whether it's the same with you?"

He tucked a loose lock of her hair behind her ear and stared into her eyes. "How does anyone ever know anything for sure?"

"I suppose…"

"That's where the trust comes in. You need to give me the benefit of the doubt if we have any chance of positively moving forward."

"And risk my heart again?" A flood of fear-laced adrenaline surged through her system.

He cupped her jaw, his thumb caressing her cheek. "We're risking a lot more already. Ultimately, it takes measured risk to achieve better results. Staying safe stunts growth. Staying safe creates stagnation, prevents finding something superior, great, perfect for you. To experience elite outcomes in life, you need to make yourself vulnerable. Embrace discomfort.

"You need to step into the unknown, the unfamiliar. Nothing too substantial, but something outside the realm of your normal sphere. If you don't, you'll remain static and unfulfilled. I know, because I've been doing that for a number of years now."

Oh. She'd never have guessed that about him. As far as the media reported, he constantly took on new challenges and thrived. Though, they were in his field of practice, so didn't encompass his whole life. "You're not freaked out?"

"Not at all. This discussion has confirmed we're even more aligned than I realized."

Lexie shifted onto his lap, leaned her head against his chest and hugged him so hard their bodies practically melded together.

He hadn't said he loved her out loud, but his words talked around, and enhanced the concept. Strongly suggested it, without outright confessing that simple, scary four-letter word.

She glanced up and met his beautiful blue eyes. So expressive, so full of emotion and the utmost intelligence. "So what now?"

"Eat something, then come to bed with me."

She laughed. "Such a man thing to say. So cliché."

"Hey, you're assuming. Maybe I just want to snuggle."

"Do you?"

"No."

Lexie laughed and shook her head. Fuck, she loved his honesty. Loved the banter between them. Not just the banter.

"But, I'll be happy to have you draped across me for most of the night. Hopefully all of it. Wake up with you in my arms."

Had this guy ever written poetry? Because he was a natural at stringing an alluring, heart-stirring sequence of words together. "And then have morning sex."

"If you insist."

She smacked his arm. "You're unbelievable!"

"I've lost count of how many times I've heard that."

She grabbed his face, his stubbled skin scraping against her palms. "You can take the man out of the city but you can't take the arrogant city solicitor out of the man."

"Something like that."

They both laughed.

"Come on. You need sustenance, then rest. We both do."

She stood and he clasped her hand. "I don't think we'll get much rest."

"Oh?"

"Don't pretend you don't know what I'm talking about. Not after what you just admitted." She exited the study door and he led her into the kitchen.

"Does that mean sex is back on the table?" he said, his tongue shoved firmly in his cheek.

"And on the bed, and maybe in the shower."

"Well, let's hurry up and eat so we can get to it."

They gobbled a piece of lasagna each, then packed the dishwasher and headed up the hallway, hand in hand.

He stopped just inside the bedroom door and hugged her to him. "Mmm…just what we need to ensure a deep, restorative sleep."

She rolled her eyes. "Is this part of your seduction routine, reinforcing the health benefits?"

"It's a fact. Hugs, and especially orgasms help. If you don't believe me, I can prove it to you. Practically. And I'm sure I can find the written research studies somewhere…" He pulled his phone from his pocket, and she clamped her hand on his wrist.

"So this is medicinal."

"And a lot of fun. The most fun way I know to get me off to sleep."

"I see what you did there."

"I hoped you would." He lifted her chin, and pressed a loving kiss on her lips.

"I need a shower."

"Am I invited?" He slipped his phone back into his pants pocket.

"Will you be good?"

"Never."

"Then *yes*, let's go." She tugged on his hand and steered him into the en suite, where they stripped off and stepped under the hot, hard spray, the heater lights warming the room.

Chase cuddled her tight, the water cascading over them. "This is nice."

It was. After the break-up of her engagement, and the associated bitterness and grief—from losing someone she naively thought she loved who supposedly loved her, and losing her beloved job— she'd been hopeful but wary about entering into another monogamous partnership.

With her forced proximity to Chase, their liaison could have gone one way or the other—grown closer or pushed them further apart. In their case, they'd both succumbed to enhanced intimacy. Physical, mental, emotional, spiritual. Professionally and personally.

She loved that what had developed suggested something deeper than a short-term sexual encounter. Sure, no-strings sex provided momentary fun but often, afterward, things got awkward. Normally someone wanted more. Knowing her and Chase were on the same relationship page provided reassurance.

Although she'd avoided a deep and meaningful discussion with him, circumstances had pushed her to express herself, and it was so worth it. Better to be totally truthful as early as possible, no matter how hard. Setting up false expectations didn't help either party. Deferring full facts until a later, 'safer' time tended to end in heartbreak.

Much to her surprise and delight, they'd reached a place of enhanced interconnection, the type, that by the sounds of it, they'd both craved.

"Let me wash your hair, then your sexy body." Chase spun her around, her back pressed against his steel-hard front. He pumped some shampoo into his palm and rubbed it into her hair, massaging her scalp. And fuck it felt so soothing, yet sent tingling, stimulating tentacles to the depths of her sex.

Chase dug his fingers in with just the right pressure. He grabbed the handheld shower and rinsed out the suds, then reapplied and resumed the scalp massage, making her moan. Continuously.

"Good?" His voice had gone all turned-on raspy.

"So good."

When he'd rinsed off the second shampoo, he rubbed in some of her geranium rose and wood, essential-oil conditioner, the sumptuous scent filling the steamy air. She'd never had a man do her hair before and it pressed all her arousal buttons. Such a simple, chaste task, yet so much sexier than she'd ever envisaged.

While he let the conditioner do its magic, he squirted body wash onto his hands and slowly, thoroughly scrubbed her body, as promised, further ramping up her desire. He reached between her legs and she leaned her head against his shoulder and bucked into his palm.

Instead of letting her come, he sudsed up his hands some more and stroked between her ass cheeks, stopping to tease her rear hole. Poking, prodding, persisting. Getting into a core-clenching rhythm.

He washed the soap off his free hand and rolled her clit beneath his fingers. One, two, three rubs, then thrust two fingers into her ass, and she came. Full. On. Relief. Heaven. Just what she'd needed after their heavy discussion.

"Fuck, that's hot." His whisper scorched her ear, extending her release.

Her legs turned to limp cooked noodles, and he wrapped a strong arm around her waist, preventing her from falling onto the shower base. "Mmm...thank you."

"Thank *you*."

She went to move, to turn around, but he stopped her.

Lexie jerked against his hold, trying to escape, desperate to suck his dick. "Let me return the favor."

"Not yet. But I promise you will."

"How?"

"Do you trust me?" His breath caressed the shell of her ear.

Did she? More than most people. Maybe ninety-eight percent. He still had to prove himself once they resolved the threat situation and returned to reality. "Mostly."

He chuckled. "I appreciate your honesty."

"And I appreciate yours."

"Good. Because I want to fuck you deep and hard, and I have just the position."

Oh. She squeezed her thighs together without thought. "In here?"

"No."

"Then hurry up and wash yourself, while I rinse out my hair, so we can give it a go ASAP."

"Excellent suggestion."

They finished showering within a couple of minutes, and the moment they were both dry, he whisked her into his arms and carried her to bed. He lowered her onto the mattress, with her butt on the edge, her legs hanging over.

Chase finger-combed his damp hair, keeping it slicked off his gorgeous face, and stood between her knees. "Feet on my shoulders."

Lucky for the high mattress or they wouldn't have reached. He towered over her. For some reason, she had always had an attraction to tall men. Tall, lean, fit guys in particular.

Chase gripped her hips and slid her further forward, then ran one hand up the outside of her leg, while he lined up his cock with the other. She'd had lots of sex but amazingly, hadn't tried this position. And she couldn't wait.

They already slotted together so well, and it intrigued her to see if this combination had any additional benefits. Lying comfortably on her back with him standing and in control, his hungry eyes roving over her, had her juicing up.

His penetrating blue gaze met her eyes. "Ready?"

"And waiting."

He rectified that instantly, slipping his dick into her well-lubricated entrance, managing to ping every pleasure point. Using slow, careful but confident thrusts, he hit the deepest spot anyone had ever reached.

Tingles exploded in her core and reverberated throughout her body, extending right to the tips of her toes. "You feel...oh..." She sighed, losing the ability to articulate her thoughts, her brain overrun with bliss.

He growled—apparently equally unable to form words—and picked up the pace, increasing the incredible friction.

She played with her clit ring, their combined grunts and groans, escalating into a crescendo, and they plunged over the orgasmic cliff. Free-falling with an avalanche of euphoria.

Their gazes remained locked the whole time, adding to the pleasurable intensity, while they came to the end of their combined climax.

"Fucking brilliant."

He wasn't wrong. She lay there panting, unable to speak, still floating on a cloud of elation.

"Stay here."

Oh, she wasn't going anywhere in a hurry.

Chase slipped out of her and walked into the en suite. She could never get sick of that view—taut ass, broad back, muscular legs. She looked forward to ogling his chest and shoulders and abs as he returned. He exceeded the criteria for the hottest guy she'd ever fucked.

Water gushed in the sink, and seconds later, he appeared with a warm, moist washcloth. He tenderly wiped her pussy clean and bent to kiss her pelvic bone, bringing back hot-as-fuck memories of their earliest encounter.

"Will this be a full repeat of our first time?"

"If you like." He stared into her eyes, as though searching for an answer. "What have I missed?"

She realized he might not remember every detail. They'd had several steamy sex sessions since their original hands-on, mouth-on interaction. "Well, you need to toss the cloth aside and eat me out."

"Do I?" He threw the flannel toward the entrance of the en suite, only a short distance away. "Let's see if I can improve on my initial efforts."

Chapter Seventeen

After a sublime bout of wake-up sex the next morning, Chase made breakfast while Lexie disappeared into the study and logged on to her laptop.

He'd promised her quiche Lorraine, and her mouth watered just thinking about it, thinking about him. Thank fuck for online shopping or they'd have been screwed, and not in a good way. After her recent jaunt into the post office, it reinforced they needed to remain remote. Together. Wherever possible. Both of them had to avoid too much exposure.

She didn't even want to think about a situation requiring regular separation. Kind of defeated the purpose of her protection detail. And she couldn't possibly take him with her. Wandering about in the community practically placed a neon flashing target on his broad back, as well as putting her in increased danger.

While waiting for the computer to load, she checked her phone and *oh shit*. A voicemail from Alex.

"Lexie, when you get this, read your emails. We've had a bit of a breakthrough in the investigation."

The moment her email program opened, she located his high-priority message.

Hey Lexie,

Make sure you thoroughly review the information I've forwarded, below. Don't skim. I need you to take in all the details and get back to me with your thoughts, so we can discuss the next important steps.

The tech team had done an amazing job, narrowing down the origin of the assailant's electronic communications to somewhere within the strip of shops in the local town. It was a massive discovery. And Alex had arranged to send a bunch of agents up to provide extra protection.

Not majorly surprising though, given the threats sent to Chase's city property, plus the shot taken at him, and now the message delivered to his bush cabin mailbox. The perpetrator obviously knew where he lived, and his general movements. Being so isolated, and given the restricted resources within the local police department, she and Chase could definitely do with some more external support.

Whoever had been taunting him had either followed them here or lived in the region. Chase had spoken to the café and grocery shop owners, as well as a range of other locals. It could be any of them. Or none of them. It could be someone from the city.

Whoever it was showed immense loyalty to Mike. Usually only a small selection of people met that criteria—a friend, or a family, club or organization member.

Bikers often fit into the organized-group picture, often considered non-blood-related family, but Mike hadn't belonged to any known gangs. So that narrowed down the tormentor to a friend or relative. But who? From every bit of intel they'd obtained, Mike had lived the life of a loner.

His foster parents had passed, and his foster siblings lived interstate or overseas. Alex and the team had tried to track down his biological parents but still hadn't had any luck. The records had vague details, registering a common first and last name for his mother—Jane Smith—and no listed father.

Was that her real name? Doubtful. Record keeping wasn't as meticulous back then, with far fewer checks and bureaucratic balances. Were his parents even still alive? And if they were, could they be behind this?

Did Mike have any full or half-blood brothers or sisters? Could they be assisting him? The Solve Security team had continued to review Mike's prison visitor log but, up until now, it had only listed his lawyer. So many questions and not enough answers.

"What's going on?"

She startled at Chase's voice, darting her gaze to the door. "What do you mean?"

"You look…uneasy. Unsettled."

"Probably because I am." She swiveled in the office chair to face him.

Chase leaned his shoulder against the doorframe and studied her eyes.

She swallowed, the reality of the findings finally hitting her like a gunshot to the chest. "The electronic threats are coming from town."

"As in, the local town?"

"Yes."

His whole body tensed. "Where?"

"Along the main strip of shops. The IT crew can't be any more specific. Either the person is moving positions when the emails and messages are posted, or they've set up some basic-level diversion software, so their exact location can't be pinpointed."

He shifted and stood up straight, ramming one of his hands through his hair. "Fuck."

"My thought exactly."

He stepped inside the room, as though standing closer to her might help them come up with a suitable strategy. "So what's the plan? What do we do?"

"Alex asked me to get back to him with any ideas. And I'll also alert the local police to ensure they're on the look-out for any suspicious activity, and be ready to respond, if needed. Other than that, it's the same as usual. Stay indoors, order any supplies online, and double check the credentials of delivery staff."

"And keep Alex updated."

"That's crucial."

He swiped his hand over his face. "Come and eat."

"I will. But before I do, anything you want me to feedback?"

"Not at this stage. I can't think of what I'd add that the Solve Security team don't already know."

"Me either." She tapped out a brief email to inform her boss of that and reinforce she'd be in contact if anything else arose or came to mind.

Alex responded immediately, informing her to expect some of the team to arrive in the afternoon. Relief washed over her like a cool refreshing summer shower. With the culprit closing in, they needed all the additional help they could get.

Chase hovered until she locked the computer and stood, then he returned to the kitchen-dining area. She followed and went to the fridge to pour them each a glass of pineapple juice. She'd never been a huge fruit fan—except for her love of pineapple on pizza—but almost everything about Chase had become addictive.

He got into chef mode, cut them each a generous wedge of quiche and placed their plates on the table. Like true territorial humans, they sat in their usual spots and started eating.

With a couple of mouthfuls left, she said, "Expect the Solve Security cavalry later today."

"Good." He cut a slice through the crispy crust. "Though, I hope they're bringing some camping gear and supplies. Space and provisions are at a premium."

"They are, but it'll be great to have some back up. I'm assuming Alex has informed them of what they'll need."

She finished off the remainder of her food, an unanswered question circling in her brain. "So, how long have you known Dan and Jimmy?"

Chase placed his cutlery on his empty plate, the knife and fork clanging, and swallowed his last bite of breakfast. "Dan, several years. I met him when I ventured into town, after I bought this place. Jimmy purchased the café about a year ago and moved into the area. I get on really well with both of the guys, have from the moment I met them. You don't think they have anything to do with it, do you?"

Chase's response totally correlated with what they'd told her when she'd run into them recently. "No evidence so far suggests their involvement, but when I went to post the threat letter the other day, they both stopped me for a chat on the way back to the car."

"Why didn't you say something?"

She hadn't meant to keep it from him but then he'd done his big lecture and things had gotten heated and the conversation derailed. "I had intended to but we kind of got off track. Then when it re-entered my mind, the more I thought about it, the more I wrote it off as a couple of nosy townsfolk, checking in on you."

"But now you think it's more than that." Deep grooves carved into his forehead.

She met his concerned stare. "I don't know. Neither of them has a motive. Well, not that we've determined. Unfortunately we can't rule out anyone who knows you and where you live."

He blew out a big breath, thumped his elbows on the table and cradled his head with his hands, his fingers tunneling into his hair. "This whole thing is a total mind fuck. It's scary and unnerving to think that people I consider acquaintances, friends, might have another agenda, might want to harm me. But I shouldn't be surprised. I've lost count of how many times I've prosecuted a criminal case where the perpetrator has been known to the victim."

She had a refreshing sip of juice. "Everyone thinks it won't happen to them, that an assailant can't be someone they know. That they're good judges of character, that their situation is different. That no way someone close could want to hurt them. But we only ever know certain sides of people, we never understand anyone entirely.

"They could have major financial or health or family issues that pressure them into decisions that they wouldn't normally consider. Extreme circumstances can create an extreme reaction. We all think we're immune to it, but are we? Given the right cocktail of events, we don't really know how we'll behave, what will make us cross that ethical line, take us to the absolute point of no return."

He dropped one arm onto the table and stroked his scruff with his other hand. "I get that certain unusual, unexpected occurrences can cause an uncharacteristic response, but I'd like to think that our core beliefs would prevent us making any harmful choices. Rule out anything that could have severe ramifications like putting others at risk of permanent injury or death."

Lexie reached across the table and clasped his free hand. "I'd like to think that too, but when people are under crushing, unrelenting pressure, it virtually eradicates their ability to think clearly and with perspective." She sighed and kept her focus on his eyes. "I'm not giving them excuses, just understanding how it can happen. And I hope I'm never in the position where I need to test out my resolve."

He intertwined their fingers. "Me too. That's why every little micro-decision is important and can have a life-changing impact. Then when mistakes are made, self-reflection can help review and refine beliefs to encourage better choices going forward. That's what I try to do. It's all part of learning and improvement so I get better outcomes."

Her skin tingled from their interconnected touch. "I agree. Highlighting trigger points and delving into why they have such a huge effect has assisted me too. My workplace injury gave me a lot of time to re-examine my life, my decisions, and ultimately what is most important."

He held her hand between both of his with absolute tenderness, absolute love, his gaze unwavering. "And here we are."

"Yes. Some would say fate brought us together."

"Is that your take?" His tone had no judgment, just pure curiosity.

"Not entirely. I believe our energy created a combined crossroad. We radiated the same wavelength, had gotten to a similar level of understanding in our lives and needed each other to provide a challenge to keep progressing, to choose the right route."

His mega-watt grin lit up his gorgeous face. "I like that. It resonates with me. You resonate with me."

"Me too, obviously." She smiled, reluctantly pulled her hand free from his grasp and stood. "I better get back to it. Sorry to leave you with the dishes."

She helped him collect their plates and glasses and placed them on the bench in close proximity to the sink and dishwasher. "Yeah, I can see how sad you are," he said with a smart-ass smile.

Lexie threw herself into his arms and pressed a super-hot kiss on his lips right in the heart of the kitchen. Fuck, this man was irresistible, as moreish as chocolate double-coat Tim Tams. A staple of her diet she couldn't eradicate. Didn't want to.

She needed a biscuit or two plus a cup of espresso coffee even more after they'd bared their souls, confirmed they wanted and needed each other, connected across every possible plane, something she hadn't foreseen, something beyond ecstasy-inducing, beyond amazing. But, currently, the delicious, comforting quiche had filled her up. Maybe she could indulge for morning tea?

Chase held her face between his big warm hands. "Go do your work. But just know, you're mine. And I'll do anything and everything to make sure I keep you."

Wow. She hadn't expected that confession. She'd come to accept he had strong affection for her, that his expressed feelings mirrored a significant portion of what she felt, but was he equally all in? Did he love her?

She praised her ability to remain open and patient enough to see the positive signs and embrace their blossoming bond. A few months ago, she wouldn't have had the capability or been in the right headspace. And even without one-hundred percent certainty of the depth of his feelings, her heart squeezed with love for this man.

Mr. Civilized, one-hundred-percent decorum, acknowledged a primitive protectiveness of her — another unexpected side of him, a side that showed he cared rather than lacked belief in her abilities — but that didn't necessarily mean love. Though, she hoped it did.

His possessive, loving words repeated in her head like a catchy song, the sentiment making her practically melt. "Awww…come and call me when lunch is ready."

He slapped her ass and she hightailed it to the study. After she shut the door, she popped her headphones on to listen to Alex's latest summary, including the most recent updates. She needed to remain fully aware of any key considerations, while the external team searched for the evasive offender.

* * * *

Chase tidied up, then plonked onto the couch to check work emails and phone messages. Thankfully, his boss had shown flexibility and empathy, given Chase's circumstances, and reassigned any urgent cases to his colleagues.

In the interim, he was allocated jobs where he could contribute background support and do any required report writing. All tasks he could accomplish remotely, without any required court appearances. And he was so bloody grateful.

Chase finished the most pressing letter, emailed it through to the lead lawyer, and went to work on homemade pizza for lunch. Simplicity, and the need for something light but satisfying had him using his mum's scone-base recipe — no yeast, and significantly less preparation time.

He pre-cooked the pizza base on high, then removed it from the oven and added passata with basil, olives, leg ham, pineapple, capsicum, onion, mushrooms, anchovies and sprinkled parmesan over the top. Kind of a hybrid capricciosa-Hawaiian with a twist.

Although many people were anti anchovies and pineapple on pizza, he and Lexie didn't fall into that group, going by their favorite pizza-topping discussion. Another surprise revelation, another subject they had in common.

He put the tray in the hot oven and set the timer for fifteen minutes. Meanwhile, he cleaned the dishes then scrolled through social media. No new threatening posts, which was both positive and worrying. But he did have Sage's regular check-in texts. He responded to those, assuring her all was well.

It'd been a few days now since he'd received any unsettling messages. He hoped it didn't suggest a bigger, more potentially devastating plan was in play.

The oven timer beeped, and he donned a heat-resistant mitt and lifted the perfectly cooked pizza onto the stovetop. Using a rolling cutter, he sectioned it into slices, and was about to call Lexie, when a banging noise had him on high alert.

He slinked to the back door to suss out the specifics of the situation before disturbing Lexie, and found it ajar, smacking against the architrave in the breeze. Maybe she'd stepped outside for some fresh air.

He swung the door wide open and stuck his head out, but couldn't see her anywhere. Odd. Maybe she had ventured into the backyard to do her daily perimeter check or for a break, or for some thinking time, and hadn't shut the door properly when she came back inside. Maybe they hadn't locked it last night? They had been rather pleasantly indisposed.

Chase closed and secured the door, then peeked into the study. "Hey, everything okay?"

She turned to him. "Yes, all good. You?"

"Great." He didn't want to worry her without evidence. He didn't want to assume anything without clear justification.

After a brief bathroom break, Chase returned to the kitchen and loaded the sliced pizza onto a platter. Once he'd lifted the last piece onto the oval dish, he placed the spatula in the sink, and something poked into his side.

"Fuck, Lexie. Stop mucking around. It's not funny."

"Turn around slowly."

Shit.

Not Lexie.

A man.

A familiar man, his whispered menacing tone unable to mask the distinct timbre of his voice.

Jimmy.

Fuck no.

Was Lexie okay? He'd spoken to her only a few minutes ago, but so much could happen in a short time. It only took seconds, moments, to change a person's life forever. For better…or worse.

Chase did as the guy requested, his 'friend's' knife jabbing into his ribs. Thankfully not enough to pierce the skin and draw blood. Yet.

How the fuck had Jimmy gotten involved in this? How the fuck had he gotten in? He must have jimmied the door. If Chase wasn't so scared, he might have smiled at the really poor pun.

Jimmy hooked his foot around the leg of a nearby chair and dragged it over. "Sit. And stay quiet. I really don't want to hurt anyone…unless I have to."

How could he get out of this? Chase subtly glanced around the room, searching for accessible knives, any sort of weapon he could use to render the Mike devotee out of action, restrain him and make sure Lexie was unharmed.

Jimmy stabbed the pointed blade harder into Chase's body, pain slicing through his torso.

Chase groaned and stumbled.

"Hurry up." Jimmy gouged deeper.

Chase yelped and folded forward, dropping onto the seat, an oozing stream of blood creating a slow-growing wet patch on his T-shirt.

Jimmy grabbed a rope from an open gym bag on the bench and wound it around Chase's arms and upper body.

He wanted to fight back, but his remaining strength seeped out along with the blood. "What do you plan to do to me?" His soft, labored voice hitched.

"Whatever it takes to get what I asked for."

"And if you don't?" He sucked in an excruciating breath.

"You won't live long enough to regret it." Jimmy tied the last length of rope around Chase's ankles.

Shit. How had this guy become such a devout Mike disciple? Sweat broke out on Chase's brow and trickled down his back. He had to know, had to try to bide his time, cause a distraction to give Lexie a heads up, a chance to inform Alex, the police. A chance to keep her safe. Assuming the guy hadn't already gotten to her. "How do you know Mike?"

Chapter Eighteen

The delicious aroma of basil pasta sauce, or was it pizza, drifted under the door. Lexie checked the time in the bottom corner of her computer screen — one p.m.

Strange.

Normally they ate lunch by twelve-thirty at the latest.

Maybe he'd gotten caught up with job stuff, as she had, and started cooking a little later. She whipped off her headphones, had a stretch, and prepared to go tease him for being so slack.

Voices.

Murmured, but distinctly different.

Had Chase turned on talk-back radio or...*fuck*. Had an intruder broken in or had he inadvertently let the culprit inside while she'd been oblivious, totally tuned into work? She had to investigate.

Retrieving her allocated service pistol from her small, compact gun safe, she clicked a full magazine into place, and pressed the slide release button with her thumb to chamber the round.

She tip-toed to the office door and eased it open. Leaning forward, Lexie looked right, left, right again, assessed the corridor as absolutely clear, then crept toward the kitchen-dining room, revolver ready to fire.

The low voices grew louder, definitely Chase and another man, the intruder still too soft to recognize. If she even did.

She swept her gaze across the living area.

Empty.

No one at the dining table either.

She peered around the corner and stifled a gasp.

Chase, tied to a chair and a man in camouflage cargo pants and a T-shirt, with his back to her, pressed a knife to her client's carotid artery. More than her client. Her lover. Her boyfriend. Any sudden move and Chase could bleed to death. She had to think through her next steps super carefully.

She needed a robust plan that reduced the risk of harm to all of them. Hard to do with her pulse racing and her mind in overdrive, determined to restrain the perpetrator and set Chase free ASAP.

"Does it matter?" The guy circled Chase, a deep, angry frown on his face.

Oh. No. Jimmy. Fuck. She scanned an assessing gaze over Chase, checking for any injuries, her eyes zeroing in on a dark patch on his T-shirt. Was that blood?

Her pulse pounded in her ears. Shit. She had to get him medical attention. She had to act as quickly as possible, the second she had even a glimpse of an opportunity.

Chase glanced up at Jimmy, twisting his head and following the guy's intimidating circuit of steps. "Yeah, it does. Who would go to these lengths to protect him?"

Jimmy came around to the front of Chase and leaned in scarily close to his face. "His brother."

"He doesn't have a brother."

"The fuck he doesn't." He huffed out a frustrated breath and waved a shaky finger at Chase. "He's my half-brother."

"Through his foster parents?"

She admired Chase's calm perseverance, his determination to obtain facts. Info that could be used in Jimmy's trial later.

"No. By blood." He stepped right into Chase's personal space, shoving the knife deeper into his neck.

Her heart hammered and she struggled to breathe, desperate to resolve this before the guy caused some serious damage. But she had to be smart, sensible, strategic. Find the right second to intervene to cause the least amount of carnage.

Jimmy stepped back slightly, continuing to hold the knife but easing the pressure against Chase's skin. "He got fostered out, while I stayed with my mum, because she couldn't cope with both of us once my dad left. Who knows what Mike had to deal with? Who knows how many other kids fought to share their short-term parents' love? Did he ever receive it? Possibly, but I don't think so.

"If he had, he wouldn't have gone down this path. If my dad hadn't taken off, and my mum hadn't prevented me from seeing my brother, maybe things would be different. Maybe he could have had a happy, healthy, loving life."

"So, you feel responsible that you weren't there for him."

"At least one of the family should have been. If I'd had a regular presence in his life, he wouldn't be in this position." His voice escalated in volume with every word.

"But you didn't know. You had no way of knowing. And even if you did, you couldn't curtail his impulses, his decisions."

"Maybe. Maybe not. What counts is I can help him now. I promised I'd make things right. I promised I wouldn't let him rot in jail. I promised I'd get him out, have him set free. And you can do that. You need to do that." He nudged the knife harder into Chase's throat.

Chase sucked in a pained breath, and she flinched. "You need to give me some time." He exhaled, long and hard and tortured. "I don't have the authorization to do it alone." One, two, three staggered inhales, and he coughed. "I need to convince my superiors." He coughed again, once twice, his lips turning a cyanotic purple. "I need to put together a strong —" He gasped. "Infallible argument." He sucked in a rattled breath. "You need to assist me. Give me details."

"Of what?"

Chase coughed, and jolted against his restraints. He took in another large, grueling gulp of air. "Whatever you think will give the powers-that-be —" He breathed in, out, as though attempting to access more life-sustaining oxygen. "More of an understanding of his circumstances." Chase coughed and wheezed, then sat up as straight as possible, blood trickling from his neck.

The pressure escalated, pushing her to act urgently. Her pulse punched against the confines of her skin, her breathing rate accelerating to hyperventilation level.

Sweat broke out across her forehead, and trickled between her breasts and down her back.

If she didn't do something soon, she'd faint and Chase could bleed out, allowing Jimmy to get away, to possibly take drastic, silencing measures to ensure his freedom.

"You need to tell them —" Chase sucked in a raspy, labored gasp. "What drove him to make the decisions that put him in prison."

"I've already explained to you. He's from a broken home, and brought up in a fucking turnstile family. I mean, no one gives a fuck." Jimmy waved his free hand in the air, the knife scarily close to slicing into Chase's carotid artery. Scarily close to causing permanent, fatal damage.

She stayed put and listened and watched, like a cat ready to pounce the moment the safest opening presented.

"Foster parents do the bare minimum, but nothing more. If the kid fucks up, the families wash their hands of them."

Sounded like their biological parents didn't do much better, possibly worse.

Chase inhaled and descended into a coughing fit. "You and Mike had a hard life, being split up, raised separately."

Such a great rapport-building response. She couldn't have done better.

"Damn straight. We did. In our own ways. I just wish I'd had the means to get him back sooner. Before..." Jimmy dropped his gaze and studied the floor, the knife still twitching in his hand. "Anyway, I can't do anything about that now. But *you* can. You can assist me."

Lexie pressed her back against the wall, right at the corner leading into the kitchen. Thank fuck the guy hadn't come to check on her and her whereabouts yet.

She tried to breathe as silently as possible, her finger on the trigger, her gun ready to fire. If needed. As an absolute last resort. How could she best manage this? If she tried to call the local police Jimmy would hear, and by the time they arrived, Chase might be dead. She had to act now.

Lexie grabbed the packet of mints from her pocket, aimed at the front door and tossed it with force. It thumped against the wood, and Jimmy swiveled to investigate. He stepped away from Chase and she fired, the bullet hitting the top of the guy's shoulder.

Jimmy cried out, the knife clattering to the timber, right before he slumped onto the floor, grasping his gunshot wound.

Chase threw himself forward, toppling onto him, pinning the perp underneath his weight. Making sure he couldn't reach his weapon or get away. Incredibly scary yet impressive move by her man.

Jimmy shouted, shoving against Chase's body, begging to be freed. No way would she let that happen. Oh, she'd let Chase loose, then between them, they'd restrain the guy until the police and ambulance arrived. But other than that, Jimmy's only freedom would entail transferring him to hospital under police guard followed by long-term incarceration.

Chase. *Her man.*

Yeah, he was, assuming he still chose her after they sorted out all this shit. Assuming he was okay. She needed to phone emergency services before doing anything else.

Lexie punched in triple zero and requested an ambulance and the police. Then she grabbed scissors from the kitchen drawer and cut through the rope binding her boyfriend. He broke free, throwing the chair off him, and keeping Jimmy pressed to the floor.

"We need to restrain him until the cops arrive." He blew out a strenuous breath and struggled to suck in fresh oxygen. "And if you haven't already, call Alex."

She raced to the study, grabbed some handcuffs and gauze from her security first-aid bag, and with Chase's assistance, while wielding her gun, secured Jimmy's wrists and ankles to a chair and patched him up.

"I'll watch over him." Chase sat by the culprit, gauze in both palms — one pressed to his bloody neck and one to his torso wound to stem the bleeding. He looked totally energy sapped and exhausted, but determined, down to the last dregs of adrenaline.

Lexie snatched her mobile from her pocket and notified Alex, while keeping her gaze and revolver trained on Jimmy.

"Have you called the paramedics and law enforcement?"

So Alex. From what she'd observed, he couldn't help but follow procedures, spout off all the technical terms. "First thing."

"Good. And you and Chase are okay?"

She met her man's intense, relieved stare. "Yeah, I think we are."

"Let me know when the police and ambulance are all done."

"I will."

Although Chase had lost some blood, he hadn't passed out thankfully, suggesting he wasn't too seriously injured. However, shock could make people appear a lot better than they actually were, which often caused them to crash.

Lexie knew all about that, following her in-the-line-of-duty incident. She'd pushed on, desperate to apprehend the assailants, thinking she could cope. Until she couldn't.

She hung up and stood by Chase's side, running her hand along his arm. "Are you sure you're all right?"

"Oh yeah." He paused, his breathing heavy, labored. "I can't wait to see this guy taken into custody." His jaw clenched tight, his words tinged with total conviction. "If I could, I'd prosecute him myself." He sucked in a wheezed breath.

"Good luck. I didn't kill anyone. I'll get off. You'll see." Jimmy thrashed against his restraints, but he wasn't going anywhere...until law enforcement collected him.

The police, ambulance, and allocated Solve Security agents arrived close together around twenty minutes later. The paramedics did a thorough check over Chase—cleaning and applying compression wound dressings on the two bloody cuts and requesting he organize a follow-up medical appointment for tomorrow—then Jimmy, then her, and gave the go ahead for Jimmy's arrest under medical correctional guard.

Two on-duty cops released Jimmy from his shackles, clapped a fresh set of handcuffs on his wrists and accompanied him into the awaiting ambulance.

Chase and Lexie sat in the living area, watching the whole scene through the window, huddled together on the couch while the remaining police officers chatted with the Solve Security team members, as they finished gathering evidence.

She and Chase didn't talk, just touched, her curled up against his uninjured side, but that conveyed everything, the smallest nuance. Body language really did express so much more than words. His care, his positive energy, his love soaked into her.

They gave their statements then, the moment all the agents and emergency services staff left, Chase stroked her cheek, his eyes focused on hers. "Let me say this without interruption, okay?"

"I promise." Bloody hard, but she'd do it, keep any questions in mind and ask them at the end.

He raked his hand through his thick, golden hair and breathed out, the air staggering from his lungs.

"I'm fine. I'm f...fine." He flinched, pressing his other palm hard to his chest. "These past few weeks have been tough, challenging. Not just because my life was at risk. It's so much broader than that."

Chase held Lexie's hand, keeping it captive, in the most loving way. "I know I said I'd do anything to protect those I care about. But I don't just care about you. I love you."

He smiled and scrubbed his palm over his face. "I hadn't anticipated things progressing to this point but... Forced proximity can go either way. Luckily for me, hopefully for us, it went down the positive path." His huge grin added to his already addictive personality.

Totally contagious. She couldn't help but smile back, and fully meant it, felt the joy in every single cell of her body. Adrenaline played a part, but her reaction exceeded a basic bodily response.

The whole result had turned out brilliantly. No one had been seriously hurt, and she and Chase had stayed together and planned to pursue a committed relationship. She couldn't wait to see what happened next. What their combined future held.

"Definitely down the positive path for me." Her voice came out all husky with lust.

"Good to hear." He kissed her forehead, her nose, her lips. "I need you to know that, as I've said before, I can't help but worry about you. The sort of work you do is dangerous.

"But, I fully support you following your passion. It's so important to do a job that you enjoy, that you're excited about, that you find rewarding. If anyone told me to stop being a criminal prosecutor, I'd tell them where to go."

"Exactly. You get it."

"I do. What's essential is to be with someone who understands my drivers, understands me, and vice versa. That we care, respect and love each other. If we have that, we can work through anything."

"We can. I agree."

Chase caressed her cheek. "So, not to pressure you or put you on the spot, but you haven't confirmed whether you love and respect me?"

Her eyebrows drew together in protest. "Yes, I have."

"You haven't said it."

"But I've demonstrated it through actions."

"Well, I need to hear it too."

Lexie hadn't said the 'L' word to anyone, ever. Not even to her ex-fiancé. She'd thought she'd shown it through her behavior, but in hindsight, she hadn't.

When she reviewed the whole situation with her ex, as hard as it sounded, she hadn't loved him. Had never felt the desire to say she did. Every time the word popped into her head, it evaporated like a flimsy, floating soap bubble.

She snuggled in closer, and stroked her hand over Chase's rough, bristly cheek. After everything that had happened, she'd learned and grown heaps. It presented an incredible opportunity for her to keep traveling along that optimistic track, that forward-moving happily-ever-after trajectory.

Did taking that trail guarantee it? No. But she needed to be on that course to even have a chance at long-term relationship success. At success in life.

Chase had exhibited a history of open expression, so she couldn't deny his request. Didn't want to. Her feelings rose up, ready to burst free. She had to say something or she'd explode.

"I respect you...now. Initially I felt conflicted. But after what we've been through, what you've done, the passion you have for your work, and mine, for ensuring justice, protecting others you care about, how can I not love you? It's impossible. I love you so much. Beyond what I thought I'd ever experience. Beyond what I thought was possible with anyone."

A beaming smile overtook his entire face. "Thank you."

"Thank *you*."

He swept her hair into a low ponytail and tugged. Gentle, yet arousing. "Let's pack up and move back to my place."

"This *is* your place."

"You know what I mean. My house in metro Melbourne."

"Oh, the big, fancy estate." She put on her best hoity-toity voice.

"That's the one. Unless you want to go to your apartment? I'm cool either way. I don't care where we are, as long as I'm with you."

Careful not to put too much pressure on his wounds, she held him harder, not ever wanting to let him go. Chase really was the sweetest, most romantic man she'd ever known. "Happy to slum it at yours, assuming they've fixed the window."

"They have."

"Great. Your place it is."

Epilogue

A soft knock sounded on Alex's study door. "Alexander, do you have a moment?"

He glanced up, his eyes bleary from a full, exhausting day, his gaze meeting his gorgeous wife, standing in his home-office doorway dressed in white, translucent lingerie that would stop traffic. Totally jolted him back to life. Like she always did.

"For you, oh yeah. But first, take that off. Take everything off." His voice came out rough and raspy and demanding. Coarse, desperate, needy. He needed Sage naked. Needed some lustful, loving physical contact.

Like always, she understood him, his mood, his emotions, his psychology, what he required, what they both required, and because he never took the piss she did as he asked without hesitation, without even a hint of a flinch. Without even a hint of resistance. Just total trust.

In fact, as she slowly lifted the sheer slip over her head, her nipples beaded, growing extra hard. And he couldn't fucking wait to touch them, tweak and tease until she moaned.

Sage threw the semi-see-through sleepwear aside, then her white lace panties, and *fuck*. Fucking breathtaking.

He'd seen her nude too many occasions to count, but she still got him hard-as-fuck every single time. Alex roved his gaze over her beautiful bare skin and couldn't wait to sink into her again.

How could he think straight now? His dick thrust against the confines of his jeans, eager to break free and make love to his woman. But he needed to concentrate, at least for a few more minutes. Listen to her, talk it through, make some notes to come back to tomorrow. If needed.

She sauntered over to him, slow, sultry, sexy, and he wanted to rip open his fly, pull her down onto him and thrust into her moist heat. However, she stopped and stood between his thighs.

"Are Chase and Lexie okay?" She searched his eyes.

"They are. They've driven back to his house in Melbourne and are all settled in."

"The two of them?"

"Apparently." Who'd have thought? They seemed like polar opposites and yet... "Just proves that assumptions mean shit."

"They do." She kissed his forehead, her beautiful breasts brushing his lips. "I'm happy to hear it. He's been alone too long. Lonely. Hook-ups don't fill that emotional void."

"Agreed. But he needed to find the right person."

"As we did."

"That's right."

She shifted from one foot to the other. "So, um, I need to speak to you about a possible job."

Damn. Fuck. She looked so serious, he'd have to hold off on ravaging her until later. He ran his hands along her slender arms. "What is it, baby?"

"An old friend, Penelope King, contacted me." Sage placed her palms on his shoulders and looked at him with a confused crease in her forehead. "I know it probably sounds extreme, not believable—I struggled to believe it—but she swears her husband, Marcus, is involved in something concerning."

"Concerning in what way?"

She exhaled, hesitating before she replied, her fingers digging into his traps. "She's adamant he's behind a number of deaths."

Alex pressed back into his office chair and studied his wife. "Deaths?" As in multiple murders, as in serial killer? Couldn't be? Could it? Penelope and Marcus were well known socialites, appeared at charity functions in the newspaper, women's magazines, and on social media most weeks.

Someone well off, in the public eye, wouldn't want to draw negative attention to themselves. But maybe he'd flirted with the blurred edges of society morals, and had gotten away with murder, figuratively and possibly literally. People with money often had connections, extortion info, as well as status, respect and power.

Who knew how many people with means got away with shit. Because they could. Because they could buy their way out of situations. Buy people's responses, backing, blackmail them where needed.

Alex refused to let anyone get away with homicide. No matter who they were. Rich, poor. Didn't matter. And at the same time, he didn't want to assume, go off a third-hand report, off hearsay. He needed to dig around and obtain facts first.

Sage held his jaw and tilted it up until their eyes met. "Yes. You probably recognize his name as a well-known businessman. From what I could find on the internet, he has no criminal record, but his wife insists he's behind a series of killings. And she's worried about who else he might target, in addition to fearing for her own life."

"Fuck." He guided Sage onto his lap, wrapped his arms around her bare body and pressed a kiss to her temple. He loved his woman, his sublime, sexy, sweet wife, so fucking much.

"Give me their details, and any other info you have, and I'll look into it. Subtly." He didn't want to put the alleged perpetrator's partner at increased risk. "If there is anything suspect, I'll have a couple of agents investigate further."

Alex would ensure Penelope's protection, as much as he could, within his restricted resources. And yeah, that sounded like a cop out, sounded like a fucking massive excuse, and it was.

One that majorly pissed him off, but no matter how unfair, unfortunately money bought options. So if she wanted him to dive deeper, she'd need to fund him to take on the case.

Given how much capital he'd sunk into starting up his new business, and paying office rent and wages, he only had limited cash left to spend. Anything outside of that, came down to providing practical advice. Nothing more.

So he'd collated a comprehensive tip sheet on how to stay safe to give to her, and others in similar scenarios. Simple things like 'visiting' a friend or a family member for a few days or taking an organized-group multi-day bus tour and relaying only vague details to potential perpetrators. Basically, setting up for less alone time significantly increased a person's chances of survival.

Sage pressed a grateful, lingering kiss to Alex's lips, laced with a fuck-ton of desire and temptation. "Thank you."

He smiled and swept a few strands of her long, silky cinnamon hair off her stunning face. "I'm just about to finish up. Go to bed, and I'll join you soon." And he meant that in every possible way.

Sign up for our newsletter and find out about all our romance book releases, eBook sales and promotions, sneak peeks and FREE romance books!

Want to see more from this author? Here's a taster for you to enjoy!

Hearts in Danger: Come What May
Sandra Carmel

Excerpt

May Caledon's car clunked and sputtered and came to an abrupt halt, steam streaming from beneath the bonnet.

Noooo! Just what she needed.

Not.

She was almost there.

She huffed and shook her head. "Great. So bloody typical." Of all the times her car could break down, it had to happen on the way to her first serious job interview. The first position that had piqued her interest since she'd left the military.

Only a short couple of kilometers away from the location, according to her GPS. So close, yet still so far. Thank fuck for mobile phones so she could at least let Solve Security know she'd be running late.

And thank fuck she knew the intricate workings of a car. With or without electronic diagnostics. Intimately understood how to fine-tune an engine.

Hazard lights on and with car horns blaring, she threw the gear stick into neutral, jumped out and steered her current labor of love to a safer spot on the side of the busy road.

Extracting a hair tie from her purse, she wound her untamable, rebellious locks into a ponytail then popped open the hood. Once she had the prop rod in place, she hitched up her skirt and leaned over to get a closer look.

The early-morning sun, harsher than what she'd expected, beat down on her, adding to the inflamed, unanticipated, infuriating circumstances.

She sighed and swept the wayward strands of hair off her sweaty forehead, the hot, merciless, northerly breeze whipping across her back.

Her classic red and black Holden Torana, affectionately called Ladybird, didn't have any of the electrics so couldn't tell her straight up what was wrong. It absorbed the unprecedented early morning heat to its detriment.

The persistent hissing haze emanating from the radiator suggested a water problem. Most likely a crack or possibly a leak. Fucking great. Just what she needed. Her limited budget hadn't catered for major car issues.

Hopefully the engine hadn't totally overheated. Like her internal thermostat, the pressure had built, teetering close to boiling. It would only take one more inconvenience and she'd blow her last gasket.

The air vibrated with the anxious hum of people desperate to get to work or wherever they were headed, on time. And halted by traffic. Fumes mixed with a humid mist, creating a fog that rose off the sun-soaked bitumen, and road rage horns blared at semi-frequent intervals.

Instead of playing into responses out of her control, she shifted into mindfulness meditation mode and focused on what she needed to do to ensure a successful interview.

Stop start.

Stop start.

Stop start.

Noxious exhaust gases, musty and smoky and sulfur tinged, permeated the environment, making her nose crinkle and melded with her already high stress.

Frizzy, curling strands of hair stuck to her face. She tried to blow them off, but they flopped back into place, plastering to her hot, perspiring, pollutant-exposed skin.

Unable to do a thing about her ruined hair, she'd have to wait to have a good scrub in the shower after the interview…if she ever made it.

Although tempted to check the radiator, she wouldn't risk removing the cap until the car cooled down. Yes, she wanted to maximize the meeting opportunity, but not at the expense of her safety. Not unless she accepted adding the high possibility of scalding burns to her already compromised condition.

Vehicles continued to crawl on by, the stifling northerly breeze buffeting her body, the tar heating the soles of her shoes like a convection stovetop. She debated whether to walk the rest of the way to Solve Security, then return to Ladybird later.

May refused to call roadside assistance—she was a better mechanic than all of them strung together. She dug her fingers into the back of her neck. What to do? She had to make a decision, and quickly. Did she set off on foot now, or stay put and wait until she could get her car running?

From a risk-first perspective, she didn't want to remain standing on the side of the road, or even sitting in her broken-down car for longer than needed, or else she'd increase her chances of being hit. Injured or possibly killed.

How many times had she heard news stories, how many times had accidental or sometimes purposeful deaths resulted from someone's vehicle breaking down on a busy highway? She refused to be another statistic. Losing Ladybird would be traumatic, but a fuck-ton more preferable than losing her life.

Maybe she should stand on the median strip and wave someone down to help her push Ladybird into an even safer side street.

No.

She shook her head. No.

Not worth it.

Who knew what weirdo might pull over?

Her current irritated, annoyed mood reduced her tolerance to fending off questionable-character advances. With her short fuse growing shorter by the second, she might lash out on a well-meaning male and be arrested for assault.

In the event of an opposite outcome, she trusted her extensive armed-forces training to enable her to adequately and effectively defend herself, if the need arose. However, in order to best protect herself and others, she should avoid both scenarios.

A car blared its horn and shot up the emergency lane, in an attempt to overtake a slow driver, barely missing the rear of Ladybird, and screeched back into the slow flow of traffic. Heart hammering, she retreated off the road onto the median strip. Not a ploy for male attention. A self-preservation decision.

She didn't need a guy in her life to make it worthwhile, to feel purposeful, complete. She didn't need him to do anything for her, other than offer his mouth and hands and cock for a good, thorough screw.

May blew out a frustrated breath. It had been too long between men.

A random, no-strings-attached fuck for fun, when she felt like it—which was most days—would do the desired trick. It ticked her sexual-relief boxes.

Nothing serious. Never anything serious. Serious turned into mundane boredom and the death of freedom. May knew from years of personal experience.

She'd tried the boyfriend thing a few times and it hadn't worked. For a countless number of reasons. If anything, it caused her more stress and anxiety. Too much emotional crap, too much pain and baggage to trudge through. She sought a mutual, enjoyable escape.

Instead of easing, the traffic congestion increased, decelerating to a super-slow crawl, the heightened pollution making her cough. She could practically feel the black specks of smog clinging to her face and arms and semi-bare legs. Inhaled it into her lungs.

She'd wait a few more minutes, reluctantly lock Ladybird, then attempt to meander her way to Solve Security without featuring as a hit-and-run news story.

An army camouflage-print Jeep rolled up in the far lane, a bunch of fresh-faced soldiers sitting in the back. Were they new recruits? Or returning after holidays, to wherever they were deployed, to further defend their country?

The military…she sighed. She'd loved it. Maybe too much. The insular, close, cliquey community had had her back. And she'd had theirs. She'd trusted her team with her life. Even though it had taken a while for her to convince the guys of her mechanical expertise. But it was worth every second of her hard slog.

Bittersweet tears burned like flaring fire behind her eyes. It had taken her months, following a few persisting over-use injuries, to finally pull the I-need-to-go pin.

Losing one of her close team members had finally rammed home the point that no one was ever one-hundred percent safe, didn't matter how well trained. That, plus burn-out, had started singeing the edges of her sanity. Not helpful, not healthy for her or anyone.

If she had any chance of a 'normal' life, a civilian existence with the possibility of children, she had to leave. Before it was too late. Opening up options provided a greater, more satisfying number of choices. Or so she tried to convince herself.

Having worked in the forces since she left secondary school, her team had become her second family. Although unsure of how she'd cope, she'd taken the scary plunge, and much to her surprise, had seamlessly transitioned into her new carefree single life. Contrary to the ex-military PTSD horror stories she'd heard.

Mind you, she hadn't tested herself in a new civilian job. *Yet*. But mounting financial pressure meant she needed to find something soon so she could live the free-and-easy lifestyle she envisaged.

Having a reasonable pension helped, created a comfortable buffer, however she still needed an additional income to pay for the accelerating high-cost-of-living expenses in Melbourne.

Going out for dinner at a pub and having a couple of drinks pretty much equaled her grocery shopping bill for the week. Not maintainable. Far from sustainable. The biggest shock since she returned to Australia.

Although still seeking the odd adrenaline rush, overall, she now needed a more supportive, lower-key life. Something with the occasional thrill but more stability. Hence her application for a Solve Security agent position.

If she ever made it to the meeting.

Her car cracking the sads — not a good start. Definitely the opposite of making a great first impression. An employee needed to show reliability, efficiency, effectiveness.

May reached into the driver's side door, snatched her cell phone from the center console and searched for the Solve Security number in an email, confirming her interview date, time, and venue. She copied and pasted the contact number into her mobile and pressed the call button.

It rang and rang and rang, and went to voicemail. "Hi, you've reached Solve Security. Please leave your name and number and a brief message, and we'll get back to you as soon as possible."

Fuck.

She summoned her calm voice, and waited for the beep. "Hello? It's May Caledon here. I'm scheduled to attend an interview at nine a.m. but my car has broken down. Just wanted to let you know I'll make it in as soon as I can. Sorry for any inconvenience. My number is…"

She hit the call end button and gritted her teeth. Eight-forty-three a.m. She should have been there, would have been there if… No point focusing on that. It wouldn't change the present situation.

The early morning summer sun had turned scorching. Already. Actually, the temperature had been unbearable most of the night, dropping to a muggy 'low' of eighty degrees Fahrenheit, and the weather bureau expected it to rise to one-hundred-and-four degrees today.

Great. She fucking hated having a sweaty, unsettled sleep…unless a hot man was involved. She fucking hated summer. She fucking hated turning up to her interview a dripping wet, frizzy-haired, grimy, flustered mess. She really had to get a reverse-cycle unit installed in her bedroom. And maybe a more reliable everyday car.

Normally she'd call a taxi or an Uber, but given Ladybird had chosen to lose her shit in the peak of peak hour, it'd be quicker for her to walk. Though she really didn't want to leave her pride-and-joy so exposed. What if someone plowed into her baby? Radiator replacement she could handle, but major bodyworks... no. Just no.

May closed her eyes and took a couple of big, deep breaths. She threw her phone onto the driver's seat, and with the steam dissipating, she bent over the engine again, earning her several honks and a couple of wolf whistles.

The short skirt—big mistake.

Was this an omen? Her morning had gone from promising to disastrous. Maybe she wasn't meant to work at Solve Security? Between the congested trudge of traffic, and the whoosh when they took off at the odd interval, her phone started ringing.

Shit.

She raced to retrieve it and answered. "Hi, May here."

Holding the phone tight to one ear, she blocked the other with her hand to filter out the persistent traffic noise, the relentless heat and racket radiating off the road.

"It's Alex from Solve Security. Got your message. Thanks for letting me know what's happening. Get here when you can. Safely. Don't rush." A firm, no-nonsense male voice, yet he exuded empathy. Caring. Gave her a good vibe.

Just the kind of employer she'd enjoy working for...if he continued to demonstrate his positive initial impression with action. Maybe the universe wanted to reinforce she should follow through with the agency.

Give it her best go. Didn't David Bowie say something about needing to step into the deep end, where your feet barely touched the ground to enable growth?

"Thanks, Alex. I'll give you a call when I'm on my way." She yelled over the line-after-line of chugging car and truck and motorcycle engines, and swiped the sticky sweat from her forehead, the wispy strands of hair from her eyes.

"No worries. Hopefully see you soon."

First-world problem somewhat sorted. Beads of perspiration formed between her breasts and trickled down her stomach. She could only imagine how shit her hair looked. Why had she even attempted to straighten it on such a sultry day? Because she'd assumed she'd make it in air-conditioned comfort to the Solve Security office.

Massive Murphy's Law mistake.

Her clothes stuck to her damp skin, and she fanned her face. Hopefully her mascara didn't decide to run in dark rivulets down her cheeks. She didn't want to turn up to her interview looking like one of those creepy nineteen-eighties porcelain clowns.

Or Alice Cooper. Great for rock and roll, but not so great for a security agent…unless the role called for it. She definitely didn't consider dress-ups a deal breaker.

May checked the time on her phone — nine-o-five a.m. — then dumped it on the dashboard and went to dislodge the prop rod.

Car tires crunched along the emergency lane.

She swore under her breath, closed her eyes, and froze.

Fuck no.

Please don't be some single, predatory guy.

Yes, okay, she appreciated the concern, the possible help, the attempt to assist, as long as they didn't show serial killer signs. As long as the 'do-gooder' didn't have some other personal, financial, or pick-up, date-me agenda. As long as they hadn't responded to her practically half-naked body on display as some sort of free-for-all come on.

"May I help?" A man, with a refined English accent that contrasted with her born-and-thoroughly-bred Aussie lilt. Nothing too full on, but still noticeable. The Queen's or in this case, King's English, if she had to guess.

Here we go.

Didn't matter how great he sounded, he could still prove to be a prick.

No matter how sexy his voice, he gave off an old-fashioned, I-must-help-a-lady-in-distress mentality. And she'd experienced that enough in her life, even more in the male-dominated forces.

Already annoyed and frustrated, she couldn't help but sigh. She only just held back from telling the 'selfless' guy to fuck right off. Men always assumed a girl was helpless when it came to cars. Assumed she'd want some big, tough, car-expert to save her.

How could she possibly know a multigrip from her mascara? A make-up bag from a tool kit? As a woman, she'd have no inkling where to start, how to fix anything mechanical. Of course she'd have no idea, and he'd have to swoop in and save the day. Massive ego trip on his part, and most likely some sick attempt at flirting.

Jaded much?

Could her day get any worse? She rolled her eyes and huffed, more than ready to tell the man, in the nicest way possible, to shove off.

May left the prop rod in place and turned.

Whoa.

Her breath caught in her chest. He was fucking stunning. Straight out of her fantasies. Very Tom Ellis, *Lucifer*. Tall, dark hair, built without being overly buff. Dark jeans, a chocolate-colored T-shirt, piercing coffee-colored eyes. And he had an amazing Jaguar F-Type R black car.

Fucking hot. Sexy. Expensive. This guy wasn't some opportunistic, I-desperately-need-a-fuck type. He had wealth. Choices. Going by his outward presentation. Not at all what she'd expected. She'd accused the stranger of assuming and yet she'd done the exact same thing.

But was he dodgy? Appearances could be totally deceiving. For all she knew, he might have hired or stolen the car. Ted Bundy epitomized attractive and charismatic and look what had happened to those who engaged with him.

She stood up super straight, her emotional battle-armor in place, and glared at the apparent good Samaritan. "Can I help *you*?"

About the Author

Sandra Carmel is a bestselling Australian author of racy, flirty and downright dirty romance novels, novellas, short stories and poetry, who enjoys stimulating herself and others with words. An obsession with *Jane Eyre*, particularly her infatuation with Mr Rochester, was a key motivator in commencing her romance writing journey. So far, she has taken the scenic route from steamy paranormal to contemporary to romantic suspense, creating provocative stories that delve beneath the surface of desire. She reads and writes a lot, frequently disrupted by her ever-attentive, cheeky cats, and sinfully amorous array of book boyfriends.

Sandra loves to hear from readers. You can find her contact information, website details and author profile page at https://www.firstforromance.com

ENTWINED PUBLISHING